**The taillights in Jade's rearview mirror were closing in fast.**

She frowned, tension threading from one shoulder to the next. The driver was going way too quickly. She flipped on her blue lights and slowed. The taillights grew brighter and her stomach dipped as she realized the person was going to hit her. She jammed the gas pedal and shot forward. However, the car behind her stayed right on her tail.

And then the lights disappeared.

"What are you doing?" Jade whispered.

The slam into her rear bumper threw her forward against her seat belt and she hit the brakes out of reflex. The wheel spun under her grip and the SUV whipped sideways. She jerked against the seat belt and slammed her head on the window. Stars flashed, the vehicle tilted on two wheels then crashed onto the asphalt.

Stunned, Jade hung suspended by the seat belt, her only thought that she and Bryce somehow missed one. The most importa...

one who wanted her de...

**Lynette Eason** is a bestselling, award-winning author who makes her home in South Carolina with her husband and two teenage children. She enjoys traveling, spending time with her family and teaching at various writing conferences around the country. She is a member of Romance Writers of America and American Christian Fiction Writers. Lynette can often be found online interacting with her readers. You can find her at Facebook.com/lynette.eason and on Twitter, @lynetteeason.

Visit the Author Profile page at Harlequin.com for more titles.

# HOLIDAY HOMECOMING SECRETS

## LYNETTE EASON

⬡ **HARLEQUIN**®LOVE INSPIRED® SUSPENSE

Recycling programs for this product may not exist in your area.

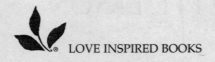

LOVE INSPIRED BOOKS

ISBN-13: 978-1-335-23251-9

Holiday Homecoming Secrets

www.Harlequin.com

**Printed in U.S.A.**

For whatsoever is born of God overcometh the world: and this is the victory that overcometh the world, even our faith.
*−1 John* 5:4

Dedicated to Emily Rodmell, my fabulous editor
of over thirty books with Love Inspired Suspense.
Thank you for pulling me out of the slush pile!

# ONE

Detective Jade Hollis pulled her unmarked SUV into the parking lot of the deserted textile mill and parked. Five minutes ago, a call had come in from someone seeing "strange lights" in the crumbling building. Even though she was off duty, she'd only been half a mile away from the address and had volunteered to stop by.

No doubt Wally Benjamin, one of the small town's homeless, had decided to seek shelter in the place once again. It seemed to be a favorite of his, and she couldn't say she blamed him.

December nights were cold—and tonight the forecast called for temperatures in the high twenties with snow. She'd pulled Wally—and a few of his homeless friends—out of the building more than once last winter and taken them to the shelter on the edge of town. Jade blew out a breath and turned off the car. The heater fell silent and she sat for a moment, dreading the idea of trading her warm spot for the frigid wind.

She grimaced. The quicker she took care of this, the quicker she could get home. At least she had a home—one that was finally in the same city as her daughter. She slipped out of the driver's seat and into the swirling snow. For a brief moment, the wind settled and dead quiet surrounded her. She heard a scraping noise coming from the interior of the old building before the wind whipped her ponytail across her face and shivers wracked her. She grabbed her coat, gloves and hat from the back seat.

After pulling everything on, she made sure she could reach her weapon. She wasn't terribly concerned about needing it but wasn't going in unprepared even though she was almost a hundred percent sure it was Wally in there.

But there'd been several drug-related deaths over the past three months and the suppliers were as slippery as eels, moving from one place to the next, never landing long enough for the police to find them and bust them. They always seemed to be one step ahead of law enforcement which was frustrating to everyone involved.

Jade carried the portable radio, ready to call an ambulance if Wally needed medical treatment—should it be Wally in the building. Last year, he'd suffered frostbite as a result of his refusal to go to a shelter on one of the cold nights. She lifted her chin, deciding the man didn't have a choice tonight. She'd arrest him for...well...something...if she had to. For his own good. A heated holding cell was better than a dirt floor in a freezing cold building that had been declared a danger zone. If it was Wally. She really shouldn't assume.

The beam of her high-powered flashlight guided her steps to the space where the front door had been. She stepped inside and swept the light over the area, then lifted the radio to call the dispatcher. "Darlene, this is Jade. Did the caller say in what part of the building he saw the lights? This place is huge."

The radio popped, and Darlene came on. "In the main building where you usually can find Wally. The person called back and said that not only were there were lights, but possibly a small fire. Fire trucks are en route."

"10-4. Thanks. But you can cancel the trucks. There's no sign of a fire." At least not in this part of the building. "Or lights." Although she did wonder what the noise had been. Rats probably. "If I'm wrong, I'll call you back." The trucks could be on site within minutes if needed.

"10-4. Stay safe."

A fire could be Wally's attempt to stay warm, but she didn't smell smoke. Jade cast the beam over the ceiling, noting it looked solid enough. Industrial pipes ran amok in no discernible pattern—at least the ones that were still attached—but the rows of spindles stood neatly as though waiting for someone to put them to work. Debris from the past littered the floor. Mostly broken equipment.

Jade stepped farther inside. Even with the gaping windows, the interior offered a bit of relief from the bite of the wind.

A click, then a scrape sounded somewhere from inside the vast cavern of space, and Jade shivered. This time, the chills had nothing to do with the weather. "Wally? You here?" Her voice echoed. "It's me, Jade Hollis."

A soft thud reached her, then silence.

The hairs on her neck spiked and her hand went to her weapon. She palmed it, taking comfort in the solid weight of it, and lifted the radio. "Darlene, send backup to the mill, will you."

"10-4." She made the request, then came back. "Are you all right?"

"I'm fine." For now. "Just being cautious. I'm hearing noises but can't pinpoint where they're coming from or what's making them." Jade backed toward the door, sweeping the light from side to side. When it landed on an old trunk against the far left wall, she walked toward it, noticing the freshly mounded dirt and large pile of bricks next to it. "Weird," she muttered. She glanced over her shoulder, straining to hear, hoping that backup would soon arrive.

A scuffle against the dirt swung her attention to the left. "Who's there?"

No answer.

"This is Detective Jade Hollis. Show yourself!"

Movement caught the corner of her eye, and Jade spun, only to be greeted with a glancing blow to the side of her head and a hard shove that sent her stumbling backward against the empty spindles. Pain shot through her as pounding footsteps faded.

With a groan, Jade rolled and fumbled for her radio.

Private investigator Bryce Kingsley hadn't planned to be in the patrol car when the call came in. He'd *planned* to return to Cedar Canyon and open his own PI business—an idea his sister and therapist had wholeheartedly approved of.

But when his high school buddy and journalist, Frank Shipman, had asked him to put the PI business on hold for a short time in order to help him with a story he was looking into, Bryce hadn't been able to say no.

"What's going on?" he'd asked when Frank had presented him with the idea.

"There are crooked cops on the force protecting those manufacturing and dealing drugs. I need your help to figure out which cops."

According to Frank's sources, there'd been two attempted stings. The first place had been emptied out before they got there. The second time was an ambush.

One DEA agent, Cooper Peterson, had been killed during the second sting.

"People know you in this town," Frank had said. "They know you disappeared for a while, so when you come back, they're going to be curious, but they won't expect you to be undercover."

Bryce got it.

"Cops don't trust reporters. I'm not saying they don't have good reasons for that, but truly, I'm not trying to hurt the honest cops. I want to take down the dirty one—or ones. Just pretend like you're trying to decide if you want to be a cop, and no one's going to protest you riding along with them."

The truth was, he'd love to be a cop, but with part of his leg missing, that wasn't going to happen.

"Frank—" He'd stopped. It could work. No one would know about his prosthesis unless he told them—or lost his balance doing something stupid. "That's not why I'm coming home. I...have amends to make." Jade's pretty face had flashed to the forefront of his mind. And then his sister's.

"All I'm asking is that you arrange for the ride-alongs and see if you notice anything suspicious. If not, fine, but something's going on with the police and a local drug ring, and I need help figuring out what—and who—is involved."

"Well, I—"

"Seriously, your job would be to keep your eyes and ears open. Make note of anything that looks suspicious. That's it."

Bryce had given up trying to argue. The truth was, his adrenaline had started to flow at the thought of the new challenge.

And so here he was. Fake leg and all. The lower half

of his left leg just below the knee sported a high-tech prosthesis thanks to an IED he'd run into six months after he'd deployed. He'd finally accepted it as part of who he was now. Finally. Most days.

Bryce shook his head even as Officer Dylan Fitzgerald spun the wheel and turned in to the parking lot of the old mill. The headlights cast two strips of light onto the building, and he shivered. It was as spooky as he remembered from his teen years. Wipers battled the snow falling, and Bryce thought they were having a harder time of clearing the windshield than they had just ten minutes ago.

From his seat, he peered at the mill. The place should have been demolished years ago. However, the historical society members had screeched at the top of their lungs about wanting to have the building placed on the registry for historical landmarks. He had no idea whether they'd done that or not, and frankly, didn't care. At the moment, his only concern was the fact that his former friend, Jade Hollis, had called for backup. Former friend? No, she'd been more. Much more. Only he'd discovered it too late to do anything about it. Two weeks before he'd deployed overseas, he'd gone to tell his sister goodbye at her college. Jade had been Kristy's roommate and her grandmother had passed away that day. He'd found her crying, meant to comfort her and had wound up sharing one unintentional night they both regretted the next morning. But it was then he'd realized just how much Jade meant to him. Too late. "Is she all right?" he asked, reaching for the door handle and shoving aside the memories.

"I'm going to find out," Dylan said. He pointed at Bryce. "You stay put."

"We've been over this. I've got training. I can handle myself." Bryce had signed a waiver absolving the department of any harm he might come to, so instead of arguing, Dylan rolled his eyes.

"Then bring that flashlight. We might need it," the man said.

Bryce grabbed the light and followed Dylan to the door just as a noise from the end of the building caught his attention. A figure dove out of a broken window, rolled to his feet and sprinted into the wooded area behind the mill.

"You see that?" Bryce asked.

"I did." He took off after the person. "Check on Jade! And watch your back!"

Bryce bolted toward the opening and stepped inside, keeping one hand on the weapon at his side. He flipped the light on and swept it around the interior. "Jade?"

"Back here." Her voice reached him, sounding weak, shaky.

He hurried to her, keeping an eye on the surrounding area in case the person who'd run had company. Bryce rounded the end of the spindle row to see Jade on the floor, holding her head. Blood smeared a short path down her cheek. "You're hurt!" For a moment, she simply stared up at him, complete shock written across her features. "Jade? Hello?" He waved a hand in front of her eyes.

She blinked. "Bryce?"

"Hi." He glanced over his shoulder, then swung the beam of the flashlight over the rest of the interior. When he didn't see anyone else, he focused back on Jade. The shock hadn't faded.

"You're here?"

"Yeah. This wasn't exactly the way I wanted to let you know I was coming home, but—"

"What are you doing here?"

"Can we discuss that later? Let's focus on you and the fact you're bleeding from a head wound."

"I… I'm all right. It was a glancing blow, but it made me see stars for a few seconds."

"Did you get a look at who it was?"

"No. I thought you were in Afghanistan. Or dead. Or something."

"Nope. None of the above." He paused. "Well, the 'or something' might be accurate." He could understand her shock. It had been six years since they'd seen each other—and that hadn't gone exactly well. "Anyone else here?"

"I don't think so."

A car door slammed. Blue lights whirled through the broken windows and bounced off the concrete-and-brick walls. Bryce helped her to her feet. "Let's get that head looked at."

"Wait." He could see her pulling herself together, the shock of his appearance fading. "I need to take a look at something."

He frowned. "Okay." She slipped away from him and went to the old trunk next to the wall. He stayed with her, and when she went still, he let his gaze follow hers. "What is it?"

"The person who hit me was very interested in whatever was over here."

Bryce nodded to the shovel and disturbed dirt in front of the trunk. "Looks like he was trying to dig something up." Footsteps sounded behind them and Bryce whirled, pulling his weapon and aiming the flashlight.

"It's just me," Dylan said, raising his hands and turning his head from the full force of the light. When Bryce lowered the gun, Dylan swiped an arm across his forehead and blew out a breath that was visible in the beam.

Bryce slid the weapon into his shoulder holster. "You catch him?"

"Afraid not. He had too much of a head start." Dylan stepped forward, brows together over the bridge of his nose. "You okay, Jade?"

"I'm fine." Her low voice pulled Bryce's attention back to her. With the shovel, she'd moved dirt from in front of the trunk. "What does this look like to you?"

"Looks like someone's been digging."

"Yes, but why? What could they possibly be looking for out here?"

"Who knows?" Bryce studied the pile of dirt and the bricks. "Actually, I don't think they were looking for anything. I think they were in the middle of *burying* something."

Bryce was *here*. Bryce. *Bryce*. The father of her child. The child he didn't know about. Six years ago, Bryce had shown up at her college to tell his sister, Kristy, goodbye before leaving for army boot camp. Jade remembered that day like it was yesterday. Just before he was supposed to leave, she'd received word her grandmother had died. Bryce had offered comfort. Then kissed her. A kiss that had led to them going too far and making a mistake that had resulted in Mia. She'd never regret having Mia, but that one impulsive action had been completely out of character for both her—and Bryce. Since then, she'd kept men at arm's length.

Jade kept her face as blank as possible, raised a brow and took another look at the scene in an attempt to gather her composure. "I think you're right," she said slowly, doing her best to ignore the pounding in her skull and the rush of memories she'd had tucked away for so long.

"But what? It's not big enough for a grave." He grimaced, and she shrugged. "Just an observation."

"Maybe it's the start of a grave," Dylan said, pulling on blue vinyl gloves. He passed a pair to Jade, and she slid off her warm thermal ones to don the others. "Let's see what we've got here." Dylan shone his light into the hole in the ground and grunted. "Looks like there's something in there."

A wave of light-headedness hit Jade, and she stumbled backward. Bryce grabbed her arm. "Whoa. Come on. We can deal with this later. Right now, you need medical attention."

Dylan eyed her with concern.

She waved a hand. "It'll pass. I want to know what was so important that someone was willing to attack me over it."

"You're so stubborn," Bryce said.

"I learned from watching you and Frank." The retort rolled off her tongue effortlessly. Some habits were hard to break.

"I think you have that backward," he muttered.

This time it was Dylan who rolled his eyes. "You two sound just like you did back in high school—like an old married couple."

Bryce coughed.

Heat invaded Jade's cheeks at the taunt.

"Not quite," Jade snapped then drew in a deep breath. She wrinkled her nose and tried not to think about the fact that Bryce was back. Here. In Cedar Canyon. One of her best friends turned…what? Turned into the biggest mistake of her life?

No. She couldn't think that. She'd do it all over again for Mia. "You never called," she said softly, her stomach knotted. "Six years and I never heard from you."

Bryce snagged her gaze. "I'm sorry."

"Sorry. Right."

So, her messages to him sent through Frank had meant nothing. He'd ignored her requests for him to get in touch with her, to call, write, send homing pigeons. Whatever he had to do, she needed to hear from him. And he'd blown her off. That hurt.

He frowned. "I was undercover a lot. On missions that…" He shook his head. "Without going into detail, communication was spotty at best most of the time."

"Of course." But he'd had no trouble staying in touch with Frank.

Dylan snapped his fingers and she jumped. "Anyone remember we have a possible crime scene here?" He glared at Bryce. "One you shouldn't be privy to."

"I have training. I was with the Criminal Investigative Division, CID, remember? And Captain Colson gave me permission. Good PR for the force and all that. So let's focus, shall we?"

Dylan's scowl stayed firmly put. Jade ignored him, stepped up to the edge of the hole and looked down. "It's clothing. Only reason to bury clothing is to hide something. Let's find out what." She looked at Dylan. "You got a bag?"

"In the cruiser," Dylan said. "Hold tight and I'll get it. While I'm out there, I'll put the paramedics on alert that you need attention."

She started to argue, but the pounding in her skull had increased to the point that she wouldn't mind some ibuprofen. "Fine."

Bryce's head snapped up. "It's hurting that bad?"

"Bad enough. The sooner we get this taken care of, the sooner I can find an ice pack."

He nodded, all traces of annoyance gone. In its place,

worry peered at her. She swallowed and looked away. So many memories were attached to those eyes. That face…

Bryce aimed the beam of the flashlight to the hole in the ground and sucked in a breath.

"What is it?" Jade asked. Dylan returned with the bag, and she took it from him. He also handed her a water bottle and four little orange pills. "Thanks." She downed them and turned her attention back to Bryce, who was on his knees, his face pale. "Bryce?"

"That looks like Frank's jersey."

Jade dropped beside him and squinted. She reached in, snagged the shirt and pulled it from the dirt. The Panthers jersey was achingly familiar. "Well, he has one like this, but so do a lot of other people. Doesn't mean it's his." Number nine. Frank's favorite kicker.

"Look at the left sleeve," Bryce said, his voice low and tight. "Frank's was autographed."

She inspected the sleeve and bit her lip. "Yeah, it's autographed."

"Then it's his."

She turned it over and sucked in hard. "No. Oh no."

"What?"

She swallowed. "Holes."

"What kind of holes?" Bryce narrowed his eyes and drew back.

"Bullet holes, I think," she croaked. "Two of them. In the chest. And…" Her tight throat wouldn't allow any more words to pass.

"And?" Dylan and Bryce nearly shouted the words as one voice.

"And," she said, "the front is soaked in blood. It's dry, but it's blood."

# TWO

Bryce turned the flashlight on the shirt. Outside, doors slammed and footsteps headed their way. Two holes, just as she'd said, with brown blood staining the front. Frank's shirt. "I saw him yesterday," Bryce said. "And I talked to him on the phone this morning." The conversation that led him to where he was now.

"Maybe he loaned the shirt to someone," she said.

"Maybe."

"Or maybe he donated it to the church fundraiser." Bryce arched a brow at her and she rubbed her forehead. "Yeah, probably not."

He pulled his phone from his pocket and dialed Frank's number, muscles tense, waiting, praying for his friend to pick up.

Voice mail.

"Hey buddy, give me a call when you get this. We need to talk." He hung up.

Jade was rubbing her head and staring at the jersey. "I'll call Heather."

"Yeah," Bryce said. "He may have gone over to her place and fallen asleep on the couch or something." He didn't think so, though.

Jade's frown said she wasn't buying that explanation, either. She dialed Frank's girlfriend's number, listened, then hung up. "Voice mail. She's probably asleep with her phone turned off. We have an early shift in the morning," she said of her fellow officer. "So, we've got a bloodstained shirt with two bullet holes." Dylan nodded and Jade shrugged. "Where's the body?" she asked. She'd voiced the question he'd been wondering since she'd pulled the shirt out of the dirt. "We need to search this place from top to bottom," Jade said.

"Officers are outside," Dylan said. "I'll get them on it right away."

Dylan left and within minutes returned with a handful of officers who started searching.

Bryce led Jade out to the ambulance and motioned for the two paramedics to take her. Once she was settled in the back, he tried Frank's number once more.

Again, he got voice mail. "I'm going to his house," he said, hanging up.

"I'd like to go, too," Jade said, "if you don't mind. If he's not there, we need to go find Heather and fill her in on everything." She flinched when the paramedic who'd introduced himself as Geoff Jones touched the side of her head.

"What'd he hit you with?" Geoff asked.

"Nothing," she said. "He pushed me into one of the spindles."

Geoff lifted a brow. "Those things have to be rusty. Have you had a tetanus shot recently?"

"Yes. It's updated."

"Good. Then just keep it clean and it should heal nicely. Let me check your eyes one more time." He shone the light in each, and she blinked when he was finished. "No concussion."

"I appreciate you checking me out, but I'm fine.

Shook up and mad that I let the guy get away, but physically, I'm relatively unhurt."

"Then let's go find Frank." Bryce held a hand out. She blinked, her hesitation lasting only a fraction of a second before she settled her palm against his. He jerked. "Your hands are freezing!"

"I think my adrenaline is crashing," she said. She glanced at the Geoff. "I'm fine to drive, right?"

He shrugged. "Sure. I don't see why not. As long as you feel like it."

"Great."

"Come on," Bryce said, still holding her hands, "let's get you into your squad car so you can warm up." He moved back, and his leg ached with that now familiar throb that indicated he'd overdone it today. Squashing the anger that was never very far from the surface, he focused on Jade and helped her get settled in the driver's seat. "You're sure you're okay to drive?"

"Why? Are you scared to ride with me?"

He huffed. "No." Bryce rounded the front of the car and slid into the passenger seat. His leg thanked him.

Dylan stepped up beside Jade's window, and she lowered it, scattering the soft flakes already sticking to everything. "I imagine the chief is going to tell you to sit tomorrow out," he told her.

"Probably. And if I need to, I will. Right now, I'm…" She sighed. "I refuse to say 'fine' one more time."

Dylan shot her a tight smile. "All right. I'm going to stay here until these guys are done, then write up my report." He glanced at the sky. "If I don't get snowed in."

"I'll do the same at some point."

"Let me know if you find Frank."

"Will do."

She rolled up her window, and Bryce shook his head. "You're one tough lady, aren't you?"

Jade jerked to look at him. "Me? Tough?" A laugh escaped her. "I don't know about tough. I just do what I need to do."

"Definitely tough. You always were."

Jade wanted to ask what he meant by that, but her heart was thumping so loudly, she wouldn't be surprised if Bryce could hear it.

Did he know?

No. There was no way he possibly could. She'd planned to tell him, of course, but time had passed, and her secret had become hers and hers alone—albeit an unintentional secret. Her parents didn't even know *everything*. "What are you doing back here in Cedar Canyon?" She put the vehicle into Drive and pulled away from the scene. It would take her a short five minutes to get to Frank's place. She doubted Bryce could tell her everything in that amount of time.

But he could start.

"It's been six years since you disappeared," she said. "Six years, Bryce, and no word. Nothing." A surge of anger swept through her and she did her best to choke it back—only because she wanted to hear what he had to say for himself.

He flicked a glance in her direction. "I know how long it's been."

"And it didn't occur to you that people would want to hear from you? That people might have things they'd like to…ah…share with you?"

He shook his head and sighed. "It did, but I—"

"You even ignored Kristy. Your own sister. She was devastated. Do you know she confessed to me that she even thought you were dead at one point until Frank told her he'd spoken to you on a regular basis?"

"It's not like I chose that path!" The words snapped from him quick as a whip.

She flinched. "Oh really? So, who chose it for you?"

"Whoever planted that IED in the middle of the road and blew up my Humvee. That's who." He slapped a hand against the dash and drew in a deep breath.

"Oh." She fell silent, waiting for him to continue, afraid he would and equally afraid he wouldn't.

"Yeah," he said.

"I'm sorry."

"I am, too."

A pause.

"Still could have called or something," she said.

He gave a short snort of a laugh. "I could have. S*hould* have, yes. And yes, I regret that I didn't, but I was dealing with *stuff*. Unfortunately, I can't change the past."

"No one can," she said softly. Boy, was that the truth. *Ask him. Ask him why he didn't call after Frank told him to.*

He pulled to a stop at the curb. "We're here."

"And so is Frank's car." The ranch-style one-story brick house sat on a one-acre plot. Thanks to the barely-there sliver of a moon, the darkness pressed in on them, making it hard to see anything but what the porch light illuminated. Brightly colored lights outlined the perimeter of the roof, and Frank had attached a gold star to the top of the chimney. Christmas was just around the corner, and Frank was fastidious about his decorations. Jade didn't have to see anything else to know the yard was immaculate. He used gardening and yard work as his stress reliever. *Saves me a ton of money on therapy bills*, he'd once told her.

"He's getting the place ready for him and Heather," she said. "Spends all of his spare time working on it. Heather helps on her days off."

"The wedding's coming up soon."

"Two weeks away."

He nodded and tapped the wheel. "I always thought I'd be in his wedding." He sighed. "Life sure does throw you some curveballs sometimes, doesn't it?" Before Jade could answer, he said, "Was he acting okay with you?"

"I guess. I see more of Heather these days than I do him. Why?"

He shook his head. "I don't know. I can't really explain it. I've been talking to him over the last few weeks, and he seemed like he had something on his mind. Like something was bothering him."

"The latest story he was going after?"

"Could be. I mean, yeah, he was focused on that, but I was just under the impression there was something else." He opened the car door and stepped out. "Let's ask him."

Jade followed him up the porch steps and waited while Bryce rang the bell. "Where are you staying?" she asked him. "At your parents' place?"

"That mausoleum? No thanks. I'm staying with Kristy and John." His parents were wealthy and retired, which meant they were rarely at home.

"Sounds like things haven't changed much between you and your parents."

"Nope."

And he wasn't going to elaborate. No surprise there. He'd never liked talking about them even as a teen. "Are the boys loving having you there?" Kristy and her husband, John, had two boys that Bryce had never met before his return.

"Of course. I'm really enjoying getting to know

them." He swallowed hard. "I hate that I've missed so much. I'll regret that forever."

At the husky wistfulness in his voice, Jade shut her eyes for a brief moment. "You could have come home sooner," she said softly.

"I know that now, but back then, I…" He cleared his throat. "Coming home wasn't an option. I'll just have to make up for lost time with them."

"They're four and eighteen months old. They won't even know their uncle wasn't there."

"But I know."

She shot a sideways glance at him. "I thought you didn't like kids."

He blinked. "What? Of course I like kids. Why would you say that?"

She stared at him. "Because you always said you didn't want any."

He sighed. "Just because I don't want any doesn't mean I don't like kids. I used to think I'd be a terrible dad, so why bring a kid into the world just to mess it up?"

"Like your dad?"

"Exactly. I mean, I get that he was super busy trying to provide a living, but as a young boy, I just wanted my dad around. And then when he was around, all he could do was criticize. Once he amassed his fortune, he was more interested in traveling than building a relationship with his kids. I grew up never knowing what having a dad was like. How can I be a father—a good father—without having that?" A shrug. "At least, that's how I used to think about it. Now? I don't know. Being around my nephews has been interesting, to say the least. And eye-opening. Kristy sure doesn't have any trouble being a good mom." He shook his head. "It's made me realize I may have been wrong about some things. A lot of things. Still not sure I'd make a great dad and don't have any intention of finding out anytime soon, but..."

It was obvious he felt strongly about missing out on his nephews' lives and his views on having children had shifted a bit, but he wasn't interested in being a father. So what would happen when she told him he had a five-year-old daughter?

Bryce rang the bell again and hunched into his heavy coat. He needed to keep his mouth shut. Since when did he just blurt out personal stuff?

But this was Jade. Beautiful, loving, unforgettable Jade. Someone he'd thought about daily since he'd left her on the porch steps of her dormitory her senior year six years ago, but he knew he didn't deserve her—because she'd deserved better than him even back then. And he'd had his own dreams to follow.

So he'd left. But he'd gone with the plan to make it up to her, to stay in touch and see if they could make a long-distance relationship work—if she was even interested. Not long after that, the explosion had ripped apart more than pieces of his body. For a while, it seemed like it had shredded his soul, too.

"Bryce?"

He blinked and shook off the thoughts. "He's not answering."

"I know. That's what I said three times." She frowned. "Are you okay?"

"No, not really." He walked to the nearest window, wiped the snow off, and tried to peer through the blinds. Impossible.

"I'm going in," Jade said.

"How?"

"With the key he keeps under the fake turtle." She

moved the piece of decoration from the mulch and snagged the key.

"He never told me about that, either," Bryce murmured.

"You weren't here, Bryce. Why would he tell you that?"

He flinched.

"I'm sorry," she said, her voice more gentle. "I'm not trying to rub it in that you weren't here. It's just that…"

"I wasn't here. It's truth. You're not rubbing it in. Forget it. Let's just find Frank."

She nodded, opened the door, and stepped over the threshold, wiping her feet on the mat. "Frank? You here?"

Bryce followed. "Hey Frank, where are you, buddy?"

Silence echoed back at them. Together, they walked through the house. "It's neat," she said, and sniffed. "He just cleaned not too long ago. Probably yesterday."

"He does love that pine scent his grandmother always used."

"She gave him a case of it when he moved in two years ago," she said. "I doubt even with his routine cleaning, he's used it all up yet."

"Two years. I missed a lot during my self-imposed exile, didn't I?"

She shot him a tight smile and moved to Frank's desk in the corner of his den. Bryce slipped up beside her to look over her shoulder. That familiar light strawberry-and-vanilla scent he associated with her filled his senses. He stepped back, and she wiggled the mouse on Frank's laptop. "Any idea what his password would be?"

"Heather?"

She rolled her eyes. "Seriously?"

He shrugged. "I don't know. Just a guess."

She typed it in. "Nope."

Bryce spotted a piece of paper sticking out of the top drawer and pulled on it.

"What is it?" she asked.

"A name. Tony Swift."

"I know him," Jade said. "He owns the shooting range where a bunch of cops practice when they don't want to use the one at the station."

"Maybe he was meeting someone there."

"Maybe." They continued the search and made it full circle back to the front door with no other information they could deem useful in the search for their friend, but Bryce was hopeful Tony Swift could answer a few questions.

"The place is spotless as always. Doesn't look like there's anything to be worried about," Bryce said.

"Other than the fact that it's the middle of the night, his car is here, but he's not home or answering his phone."

"He could be asleep in a hotel with his phone turned off."

"Why?"

"I have no idea. You're right, it doesn't make sense. I was just hoping…" He paused. "Let me check his closet. Maybe he had a last-minute trip and he just didn't bother telling anyone." He didn't believe that, but…

Back in Frank's bedroom, Bryce opened the closet door and hope dissipated. Jade stood at the entrance to the room, her expression anxious. "Suitcases are here," he said. He riffled through the hanging clothes. "And his jersey's missing." The bad feeling he'd had earlier when Jade had pulled the shirt from the dirt returned full force.

"Could be in a drawer," she said.

Bryce shook his head. "He hangs it. At least, he used to hang his jerseys. He wouldn't change his habits now."

"He could have—"

"No, he couldn't have. He hangs it up. You remember in high school, he had those two jerseys? He always hung them up. He wouldn't do anything different now."

She drew in a deep breath, obviously looking for her patience. "I was going to say, he could have worn it and tossed it in the dirty clothes basket."

"Oh, right. Sorry." He could have. Bryce stepped into the en suite bathroom. The empty hamper mocked him. He checked every drawer and under the sink. "It's not there. Washer and dryer are empty, too."

Her shoulders slumped. "I'm out of ideas, then." Her eyes met his. "I'm scared, Bryce."

"Ping his phone."

She bit her lip and nodded. "Okay." She put the call in to dispatch and asked for the information.

Then hit the speaker button.

Bryce waited, impatience clawing at him. Finally, the operator came back on the line. "I'm sorry, Jade, I can't get a signal on the phone. It's either turned off or the battery's dead."

"Thanks. I appreciate you trying for me." She hung up and pressed her fingers to her eyes. "I really don't like this."

"Me either. Let's go wake Heather."

# THREE

Heather opened the door on the third knock, her bleary blue eyes blinking rapidly. Jade noticed she held her service weapon in her right hand. "Jade?"

"Hi, Heather," Bryce said.

"Bryce? Bryce Kingsley?" Heather launched herself into Bryce's arms and hugged him. He returned the hug until Heather leaned back and cupped his face. "Wow, is that really you?"

"It's me."

"Frank said he'd been talking to you and that you were coming home to open a PI business."

"Yeah. At some point."

"Well...um...it's good to see you."

Heather gave him one more hug, then motioned them inside. Jade swallowed as Bryce shut the door behind him. She didn't want to admit she was a little jealous of Heather's enthusiastic greeting. She'd wanted to do the very same thing when she'd first seen Bryce in the mill. Throw herself against him and hug him, run her hands over his features and reassure herself that he was real. But she hadn't. The fact that she'd wanted to scared her silly. Bryce had walked out of her life and she'd managed to survive. The fact that he was back in it didn't mean anything had to change.

*You're lying to yourself. Everything's going to change.*

It was just a matter of when. But there wasn't a thing she could do about it right now.

Heather set her gun on the counter just inside the door to the kitchen that was next to the small foyer, where they now stood a bit awkwardly. "What are you guys doing? It's the middle of the night." Her eyes sharpened. "What is it? What's wrong?"

"We hope nothing," Jade said. "Let's go into the den and we'll explain."

"No," Heather said. Jade froze at the sharpness and Heather held up a hand. "Sorry. Can we go in the kitchen, please? I've torn up the floor in there to start fixing the place up to put it on the market. Frank and I don't need two places. And besides, I'm thirsty."

The three of them took a seat at the kitchen table while Heather retrieved water bottles from the refrigerator.

"Tell me what's going on," she said, unscrewing the cap and taking a long swig from the bottle.

Jade explained about the attack at the old mill and finding the jersey with the autograph on the left shoulder. "It has to be Frank's," she said. "Do you know where he is?"

"Well, before you asked, I would have assumed he was home in bed. Obviously he's not." She rubbed her eyes, a slow fear building in them. "What are you not telling me? Is he okay?"

"We're not sure," Jade said. She should have known better than to try to leave out details. "That jersey we found at the mill? It…ah…it had two bullet holes in the front and is covered with dried blood."

"What?" Heather paled. "His Panthers jersey?"

"Yes."

"But...no. It can't be his." A short, humorless laugh escaped her. "I mean, he just wore it the other day." She snagged her phone from her robe pocket and tapped the screen. From her seat, Jade heard it go straight to voice mail. "Frank, this is Heather. I know it's the middle of the night, but I don't care. Call me as soon as you get this message." She hung up and tried four more times before she finally set the phone on the table and clasped her hands in front of her. Her gaze bounced between Jade and Bryce. "There's got to be some explanation." She stood. "I'll get dressed and head to his house."

"We've already been there," Bryce said, and Heather froze. "I'm sorry, Heather, but he's not there."

"But his car is," Jade said. "I know that when he flies, he sometimes takes a car service, but I don't recall him saying anything about taking a trip anytime soon—outside of your honeymoon."

Heather shook her head. "No trips scheduled. At least, none that I know of. Every so often he takes off and calls me from the road if it's a last-minute thing with the paper, but—" She checked her phone. "Nothing but your missed calls. He's got to be here in town somewhere." She raised her brows. "Or he went to see Lisa." His sister lived an hour away in Charlotte. As soon as the words left her mouth, she was shaking her head. "But he would have taken his car, so that can't be. And he would have left me a message that he was going." She paced from one end of the kitchen to the other, arms crossed, features taut and pale. She turned. "What about his office?"

Frank worked out of the newspaper office downtown. Jade nodded. "But he'd still have to drive."

"Unless one of his coworkers picked him up."

"Let's find out," Bryce said. "You have their numbers?"

Heather's lips quirked even though the action didn't reach her eyes. "I'm a cop. I don't think getting their numbers is going to be a problem." The smile didn't last long. "But I'll call his boss. If anyone would know what Frank was up to, it'd be him."

"If Frank told him," Bryce muttered.

Heather scowled. "Why would he not tell him? His boss is the one who approves the stories that he works on."

"I'm not sure he was working just one story."

"Then his boss can tell us that." Heather dialed the man's number and waited. "Hi, Larry, it's Heather." She tapped the screen to put him on speakerphone. "I'm so sorry to wake you, but I have reason to believe that Frank's in trouble. Can you tell me if he had to go out of town suddenly?"

"Ah, no, not on the paper's dime." He cleared his throat. "What makes you think he's in trouble?"

Heather explained. "What was he working on?"

"A couple of things. Nothing I can discuss with you. I'm sorry."

"Larry—"

"No, I'm not budging on that. Frank's probably just looking into something. And truthfully, he didn't tell me a lot of details, just that he was on to something big and hoped to have the full story on my desk sometime next week. Seriously, Heather, he'll most likely turn up when he's good and ready. Now, go back to sleep and quit worrying."

*Click.*

Heather slumped, frustration stamped on her drawn features. "Okay, that was a dead end. Hold on a second."

She left and returned with her laptop. "Coworkers would be the next step, right? Let's see who we can find that might be able to tell us something useful."

Thirty minutes later, they were no closer to having an answer about Frank's whereabouts, and Heather's emotional state had quickly gone south. She turned to Bryce. "What was he working on?"

"I'm not at liberty to say. He asked me not to."

"Well, he's not here, so..."

"I can't. I gave him my word that I'd keep his confidence."

"Is it something that could land him in trouble? At least tell me that."

Bryce sighed. "Yeah. If certain people discovered he was doing some snooping into their business, then they wouldn't be happy about it. But I don't see how they could know."

She snapped her lips shut. "He never said he was doing anything dangerous."

"He was protecting you," Jade said softly. "He didn't want you to know he was putting himself in that kind of situation because it would have distracted you."

"So, *you* know what he was working on?" Heather asked.

"No. I just know if it was something dangerous, he would have kept it from you. You and I walk into potentially dangerous situations every day. He wouldn't want you worried about him, too."

Heather shook her head and lasered Bryce with a hard look. "It's up to you to help us find him."

"Heather—"

Her friend lifted her chin and gave Jade a stony glare. Jade sighed and snapped her lips shut. There wasn't any sense in telling Heather there would be no "us." Heather wouldn't be working the case. If there even *was* a case.

In her mind, there was. All evidence pointed toward Frank being missing. Or worse.

"I've already said more than I should have," Bryce said, "but I'm worried."

"So am I." Heather rose. "I'll be back in a minute."

"Where are you going?" Jade asked.

"To get dressed, then I'm going to find my fiancé." She paused. "Stay in here, will you? Like I said, the den's a mess." She blew out a breath. "And I know that's just not important right now, but it's a stressor."

Jade held up a hand. "We'll stay here."

"Thanks. I'll be right back."

True to her word, Heather returned to the kitchen in record time, dressed to face the day. After several more unproductive phone calls, she dropped into the nearest chair and raked a hand through her still mussed hair. "What are we going to do? We've called everyone. His sister hasn't heard from him since he stayed over at her house last weekend. His parents talked to him yesterday, and he didn't say anything about going on a trip. Where could he be?"

Jade stood. "I think it's time to put a BOLO out on him and get help."

"I agree," Heather said with a slow nod. "I'll do it."

While Heather made the call, Jade walked over to stand in front of Bryce, who leaned against the sink, sipping his second cup of coffee. "What was he working on, Bryce?" she asked softly. "We need to know so we have some direction."

Bryce set his coffee down and pursed his lips. "He made me promise not to say anything. I don't want to betray that confidence."

"Not even if it means helping us figure out if he's in trouble or not?"

He closed his eyes, obviously torn. "What if I tell you and he's fine?"

She planted her hands on her hips. "What if you don't tell me and he's in trouble?"

More than anything, Bryce wanted to tell her, because not for a moment did he think she would be involved in what had Frank investigating the local police department. It wasn't that he didn't trust Jade. Rather, it was a matter of confidentiality.

But she was right.

What if by keeping his promise, he was putting Frank in further danger? He couldn't think how that might be, but...what if?

Before he had a chance to decide what he should do, Heather returned to the kitchen. "The BOLO is out and my brain is so scrambled, I can't for the life of me think what we should do next. How's that for being a detective for you? I'll never judge family members of a missing person ever again."

"You should stay here," Jade said, "in case Frank shows up. Bryce and I will call you if we find him. And you call us if you hear from him."

"Just sit here and worry?" Heather scoffed. "Not happening."

"Come on, Heather, you know you need to stay. Just in case he shows up."

"He's not going to show up here, I don't think. He'd go home."

"Well, you can't go there. If he's truly missing, his house will be treated like a crime scene. Bryce and I were careful, but even our searching may have disturbed something. Don't add to it." She knew she sounded bossy, but she also knew Heather might be tempted to throw caution to the wind in her desperation to find Frank.

Heather pursed her lips and looked like she wanted to argue, but finally nodded. "If I decide to go over there, I won't go inside. I may just sit and watch the house."

Jade nodded. "If you feel like you have to be there, then yeah…okay. I don't think we're going to be doing much of anything else tonight."

Heather hesitated, then gave a groan and a nod. "Fine. But please stay in touch."

"Absolutely."

"Okay, so, tomorrow…we need to what?" Heather gave a short laugh. "See? I told you I couldn't think."

"We need to find out where he was last seen."

Heather rubbed her forehead. "No one seemed to be able to tell us that," she muttered.

"I talked to him on the phone around ten o'clock this morning," Bryce said. He glanced at the clock. "Or, rather, yesterday morning. So we just need to find anyone who saw him after that."

"Heather," Jade said, "why would Frank have Tony Swift's name written down? Was he meeting with him for something?"

"At the shooting range?" Heather shook her head. "I don't know. He didn't say anything to me if he was. He could have just been practicing."

"True." Jade looked at her watch. "All right. I need to grab a couple of hours of sleep before we get started looking for him again—assuming he doesn't show up in the next little bit."

Heather nodded. "I won't be able to sleep, but I can make a list of more people and places to check with."

"Do you want me to stay here?" Jade asked. "I can crash on your couch."

"No. It's not that comfortable. We're getting a new one, but not until after the wedding. Just go home. You have to help your mom in the morning with the kids anyway, don't you?"

"Kids?" Bryce asked. "Are your parents still taking in foster children?"

Her face blanked for an instant. Then she nodded. "They are." She rubbed her eyes, then narrowed them at her friend. "Are you sure you're going to be all right?"

"Yes. Go and help your mom. I think we should get some sleep if we can. None of us will be any good if we're so tired we get sloppy and miss something. Besides, there's probably some logical explanation for where he is. Missing sleep isn't going to help finding out what that is."

She had a point, but Bryce was itching to keep looking. The only lead they had was the shooting range. He glanced at his watch. Three o'clock in the morning. It had been seventeen hours since he'd talked to Frank, and he needed to know his friend was okay. Even if he went back to his sister's and tried to sleep, he knew he'd be tossing and turning.

He kept his mouth shut until they were back in her vehicle, but once he clipped his seat belt, he said, "I want to go find Tony Swift, ASAP."

She gave a slow nod. "I was thinking the same thing. Let me see if I can call him and give him a heads up. No need to wake the whole family." Using the laptop mounted on the dash to her right, she pulled up Tony's license and noted the address. Next, she dialed his number.

"Hello?"

The groggy Southern voice came through the squad

car's Bluetooth. "Tony, this is Detective Jade Hollis with the Cedar Canyon PD. I'm so sorry to be calling this late, but we're looking for Frank Shipman. Can you tell us the last time you saw him?"

*Click.*

She frowned and lifted a brow. "Well, okay, then."

"Call him back."

She did and it went straight to a busy signal. She tried his cell phone and got voice mail. Bryce locked his gaze on hers. "I don't like the implications of that."

"I don't, either. I think we should head over to his house." She cranked the car and backed out of Heather's drive.

"You think Frank's alive?" Bryce asked softly.

"I don't know, Bryce. You saw what I saw."

"Two bullet holes and all that blood doesn't give me much hope."

"It might not have been him wearing it," she said. "That's what I'm holding on to—and feeling guilty for doing so. I don't want Frank to be hurt or dead, but I don't want anyone else to be, either."

"And yet, it's highly likely someone is."

"Yeah. Someone is."

But who?

Jade slipped her weapon into her holster and rubbed her bleary eyes. Last night she and Bryce had found Tony Swift's wife home alone. "I don't know where he went," she'd said. "Just bolted out of here like his tail was on fire. Didn't even take his cell phone."

So now, Jade planned to show up at the range and hope he had the good sense to be there. As much as he loved his business, he wouldn't just leave the place un-opened. She hoped. She'd already talked to her supervisor and he'd given her his approval for her plan for the day—after making sure she didn't need to take the day off. As if she could. Heather had texted that Frank hadn't shown up and she still couldn't get him to answer his phone.

Little arms wrapped around her legs and her heart lifted. She turned and scooped her five-year-old daughter into a gentle hug, and she breathed in her sweet scent. "Good morning, little bear."

"Morning," Mia said. "I want eggs and bacon."

"I think that can be arranged since that's what I smell cooking all the way over here."

Mia sniffed. "I don't smell it." She smacked her lips. "But I can almost taste it. And pancakes."

"Wonderful."

"And I want to decorate for Christmas. When can we do that?"

Jade smothered a small groan. It wasn't that she didn't want to decorate. It was just the energy decorating required. Energy she was lacking right now thanks to a still twinging head. It wasn't pounding, but it didn't feel great, either. "We need to do that, don't we?"

"So, when?"

"How about tonight?"

"We can go tree shopping?" Mia asked, her eyes widening, her joy practically tangible.

"Well, as long as you bundle up really good."

Mia frowned and wrinkled her nose. "Oh, right. It's very cold outside, isn't it?"

Her daughter had no use for cold weather. "Well, yes," Jade said, "it is. What about if I just come home with the tree and you and the twins can help decorate. Is that okay?" Her heart ached for Jessica and Gage, the ten-year-old twins who'd been removed from their home and placed with her parents a little over four months ago due to neglect.

Mia nodded. "It's okay with me. I don't really care about getting the tree, I just want to make it pretty. I'll ask Gage and Jessica. If they want to go, you can take them. Can we string popcorn?"

"If you can manage not to eat it all." She tickled the little girl's ribs, and Mia's giggles soothed her worried heart. "Are Jessica and Gage ready to eat?"

"They're always ready to eat."

That was true. Jade gave thanks that they were good-natured children in spite of everything they'd been through and had adjusted well to the routine of the home—managing to steal all of their hearts in the process.

Last week she'd learned the twins' parents had finally released them for adoption. Her parents had talked to Jade about plans to adopt them, and Jade thought it was a fabulous idea. She just hoped the twins did, too. They were happy here and made no secret of that.

Of course, the fact that there were horses on the property didn't hurt. Jessica had already attached herself to Belle, one of the horses her parents used to teach the kids to ride. "Tell Lolly, I'll be there in just a few minutes." Jade's mother was named Adelaide. When Mia started talking, all the child could manage to wrap her tongue around was Lolly. Her mom had been fine with that.

"Okay." Mia ran down the hallway toward the stairs, her long, dark hair flying around her head. She'd go down the steps and out the bottom door that led to an enclosed walkway. At the end of that was her parents' kitchen. Her father had closed in the area about six months ago so Mia could travel between the houses without having to go outside—and ease Jade's mind about keeping a constant eye on her when she wanted to see her grandparents. "All by myself. I can do it, Mommy."

Her little girl was growing up.

Jade's throat tightened as she thought about telling Bryce he had a child. It was obvious he had no clue about Mia. Which was the way she'd originally wanted it. But then she'd felt so guilty about keeping that secret, she'd done her best to get in touch with him. Her only source had been Frank. She'd asked him to let Bryce know she really needed him to call her. Frank had said he'd told him. Obviously, Bryce hadn't deemed it important to do so. Which really hurt. And made her mad. Maybe she should just ask him and give him a chance to explain before giving up on him. Maybe.

But first things first.

She'd wolf down the food, then head over to the shooting range and hope Tony had come to his senses. If not, she was going to have to sit down with her chief and other investigators and figure out a plan of action.

For now, she'd have breakfast with Mia, Jessica and Gage. She made her way to the kitchen and found everyone gathered around the table.

"Jessica and Gage said you could get the tree and bring it home. They don't want to get cold, either."

Jade smiled. "All right. Sounds like a plan."

"Glad you could join us this morning," her mother said.

"There's no way I'd miss this spread." Eggs, bacon, sausage, grits and biscuits. Her mother's heritage might be Korean, but she cooked straight Southern when she was in the mood. "Unfortunately, I'm going to have to rush through it, though." She took Mia's small hand in her right and Jessica's in her left. "I'll bless it." She said a short prayer and, after a round of amens, looked back to her mother. "Where's Dad?"

"He's already eaten. He had to go move the horses to the south pasture so they could start clearing the land for the new barn."

In addition to raising foster children, her parents boarded and raised thoroughbred horses. Each week seemed to bring one or two new clients. A good problem to have, but a lot of work as well. "I'm sorry I can't help him."

"He's got help. Eat your food, then go do that job you're so good at." She paused. "I thought today was your day off."

"It is. Was. I've got some things I need to take care of that won't wait. But I'm hoping it will be a short day." Somehow she doubted it. Not with Frank still missing. But she could hope—and she had to bring a Christmas tree home. She winked and turned to the children. "Eat up, little people. The bus will be here in thirty minutes. And don't forget, we're pulling out Christmas decorations. You can start when you get home from school. It's the last day before break and you don't want to miss all the candy that will be passed around. And cake at the party."

"And Christmas games," Jessica said with a shy smile.

"Sounds like a perfect day to me." Jade brushed the bangs from the girl's eyes and tapped her nose. "It's going to be fun."

The children cheered, and Jade's mother grinned at the happiness at her table.

Jade hadn't told her parents about Frank. It had been so late when she'd finally slipped into bed that she hadn't had a chance. And no time this morning. Not in front of the kids. They adored Frank—especially Mia.

"Lolly?" Jessica's hesitant voice caught Jade's attention as well as her mother's.

"What is it, darling?" Her mom paused to give the child her full attention.

"Are we going to be here for Christmas?"

"Well, now, that's a really good question." She sighed. "I wish I could say a one hundred percent yes, but you know how this system works as well—or better—than I do."

"Oh." Jessica looked back at her plate, her shoulders slumping.

"But we sure hope you will be," Mia said.

"Me too," Jessica mumbled around a mouthful of bacon.

Gage's bright gaze bounced from one person to the next. "I'm staying here. I don't care what anyone else says."

"We'll see," Jade said. "Just know that we all want you here more than anything."

"Absolutely." Her mother gave a firm nod.

"Thanks," he whispered.

Jade's heart stuttered with love for the little boy and his sister. She caught her mother's eye and saw a sheen of tears hovering there just before she looked away. Bless her. Such a tenderhearted woman. All she wanted was to make the world right for kids who didn't know what it was like to have that happen. And so did Jade. "I'm going to stop by my office first, then pay a visit to someone I need to question about a case."

Fifteen minutes later, with her mind on Frank and Bryce and trying to keep all of her emotions under control, Jade kissed her mother and daughter goodbye, gave hugs to Jessica and Gage, and took off for the station, praying she could dig up something that would tell her where Frank was.

# FOUR

Bryce opened the door to his sister Kristy's kitchen, and his dog, Sasha, darted around him to shake the snow from her coat. "Sasha, stop!" The dog did, but it was too late. She'd splattered melted snow everywhere. He grabbed the hand towel from the rack and made a futile effort to wipe her down.

Kristy entered with eighteen-month-old Liam on her hip. When the child's gaze landed on Sasha, he squealed. "Doggy!"

"Shh. You'll wake up your brother."

"My doggy!"

Kristy rolled her eyes. "Wet doggy." She walked into the laundry room, returned with two bath towels and shoved them at Bryce. "Messy doggy."

"Thanks," he said. "Sasha, sit." The dog obeyed, and Bryce draped the first towel over her and rubbed. "She decided it would be fun to roll in the snow."

"Of course she did. Which means she brings in a gallon of water just on her fur. You couldn't get something like a schnauzer or a Chihuahua, could you?"

He raised a brow. "Really? You can see me with one of those?" He finished with Sasha and turned to the walls and pantry door.

"I guess not. What are your plans today?"

When everything was dry, he tossed the towels into the laundry room and told her about finding a lead into Frank's disappearance. "So I'm going to rinse off, change and head over to the shooting range."

Her gaze dropped to his prosthetic, the curved one that allowed him to run without falling over. "I forget you have that most of the time."

"That's one of the nicest things you've ever said to me."

"Well…that's kind of sad. I'll work on it. There's a ham biscuit in the fridge if you want to warm it up."

"I'd love it, thanks."

Her expression softened and she hugged him. "Go change your leg—you do realize how weird that sounds— and I'll pour you some coffee. You can warm up the biscuit when you get done."

"Thanks, sis." He kissed her cheek and blew a raspberry on the baby's, then headed to his room.

Once showered and changed, he returned to the kitchen to find Liam in his high chair and Kristy feeding him ham, eggs and little pieces of biscuit. Sasha lifted her head and watched him, tongue lolling from the side of her mouth.

Bryce shook his head, grabbed the biscuit from the fridge and popped it in the microwave. "She's such a slug."

"She's a monster."

"A monster in body, but she's pure love in that big heart of hers. I don't know what I'd do without her." The microwave dinged and he grabbed the food. "I appreciate you letting us stay here. I know it's not convenient."

Kristy sighed. "We're happy to have you here. We've missed you."

Liam tossed a piece of ham straight at the dog. Sasha snagged and gulped it, then turned pleading eyes on the child as though begging him to do it again. "Hey, Sash, you already had your breakfast." He chucked the baby on the chin. "You need to eat yours."

"Doggy eat it."

"You eat it."

"No no."

"Yes yes."

Liam giggled, his little teeth glinting. "Doggy."

Bryce raised a brow at his sister. "I'm not going to win this one, am I?"

"Nope."

"Right." He glanced at the clock. "I need to get going."

Kristy set the baby on his feet, and he went to Sasha and climbed on her back. "Horsey. Go."

Sasha settled her head between her paws and Bryce thought the dog almost smiled. She loved kids. His sister loved kids. *Her* kids. A pang hit him. Ever since moving into his sister's home, his vow to never have children kept slapping him in the face, making him wonder why he and Kristy had turned out to have such different views on their ability to raise children. "Hey, sis, could I ask you a question?"

"Of course."

"How come you didn't have any reservations about getting married and having kids?"

She frowned. "What do you mean?" She wiped the tray down while Bryce tried to think of a way to explain it. "I mean, motherhood comes so naturally to you. You're nothing like our mother, and I don't understand how that can be when you had no example of what being a good mother was supposed to look like."

Kristy blew out a low breath. "But I did have examples."

"Who?"

"Ladies in the church, people I worked with, friends." She shrugged. "I don't know. I just knew that our parents were the outliers, not the norms. I knew most people loved their kids and wanted the best for them—and I vowed if I ever had kids, I'd be the complete opposite of our parents and I couldn't go wrong."

He snorted. "Do the opposite? I suppose that makes sense in some weird way."

"Of course it does." She walked over to rescue Sasha's fur from Liam's mouth. "And if you ever have kids, you'll be a great dad."

"How do you know?"

"I've watched you come to love my two. And you love your dog."

"Dogs are easy to love. They don't talk back."

"True, but I still don't think you have anything to worry about when it comes to fatherhood."

"Well, it's not like I have to worry about it anytime soon, but what if you're wrong? What if there's something lacking in me?"

She sighed and walked over to press a kiss to his head—much like a mother would. "I'm not wrong, but I guess that's something only you can figure out."

"That's not very helpful."

Kristy smiled. Then frowned. "I hope something turns up today on Frank. I'm worried about him."

"Same here."

"Tell Jade I said hi."

"I will."

Bryce tapped his thigh and Sasha rose to her feet. She

followed him to his SUV, and he let her into the back seat. "Say your prayers, girl. We've got a friend to find."

When Jade pulled into the parking lot of the shooting range, she was glad to see the Open sign flashing bright red. At the station, she'd written several reports and done some research on Tony Swift, giving him time to open the range before she swooped in to question him.

An avid hunter and outdoorsman, he'd opened the range a little over five years ago. He had no record and appeared to be an upstanding citizen. So why had he run last night?

Jade parked and climbed out of the cruiser, her gaze scanning the area.

The light gray pickup truck sitting in the spot near the door encouraged her to think that Tony was inside. She pushed through the barred glass door and let it shut behind her. Tony looked up from his spot behind the counter and for a moment, she wondered if he was going to take off running. Then he sighed. "What do you need Jade?"

"You hung up on me last night."

"You called me at three o'clock in the morning!"

"And you left the house shortly thereafter." Her unruffled responses seemed to worry him. "Wanna tell me why?"

"Not particularly."

"Come on, Tony. Did you really think that I wouldn't show up this morning?"

With another dramatic sigh, he grabbed a rag and swiped the immaculately clean glass counter. "I knew you'd show up."

"So…what? You were just buying time to figure out what story you were going to tell?"

His cheeks flushed a bright red, and his startled glance confirmed her suspicions. "You're not a liar, Tony." Not a good one, anyway. "What do you know about Frank?"

He shot a nervous glance at the door. "Not a lot. You said you were looking for him. I don't know where he is, but if he's missing, then I guess that means he made the wrong people mad—and I don't have any desire to do the same."

"And who are the wrong people?"

"Whoever he was investigating."

The door chimed. Tony flinched, and Jade spun to see Bryce step inside. He shot her a deep frown. "I thought you were going to wait on me to do this."

She blinked at him. "Why would you think that? You're not a cop."

"I'm Frank's friend and I've had training in investigations, remember? I want to help."

"We'll discuss that later." She glanced at Tony. "What can you tell us about the people Frank was investigating?"

"Nothing."

Right. "Well, why did he have your name on a piece of paper in his desk drawer?"

"I guess he was going to come shooting sometime. How do I know?"

She paused, trying to find a way through to him. "What was Frank to you? Did he come shooting here a lot?"

The man blinked. "Yeah. I mean, sometimes. Not like on a regular basis, but every so often when he had something on his mind." He paused. "Come to think of it, he was in here quite a bit in the last few weeks."

"So, he had something on his mind?"

"Yeah, I think so."

"Like what?"

"Don't know."

More like he wasn't saying. "Look, Tony, Frank's a good friend and we really need your help to find him." Jade held on to her frustration with effort.

A flash of frustration darkened his eyes—along with a hint of fear. Then he sighed. "I don't know a whole lot, just that he was looking into people who didn't want to be looked into, you know what I mean? He—"

The door chimed, and two young ladies in their mid-twenties walked in, each carrying a case that held their weapons. "Hey, Tony," the taller one said. "We're here to practice."

"Excuse me." He went to help the women, and Jade spun to confront Bryce.

"You could make this a lot easier if you would just tell me what Frank was having you help him with."

Bryce hesitated, obviously agonizing over the decision, then seemed to make up his mind. He motioned her to the corner of the store farthest away from Tony and his customers. "He thought there were dirty cops in the department."

Jade gaped. "He what?"

"Shh!"

"What made him think that?" she whispered.

"He didn't go into a lot of details, just that he thought there were some cops on the force who didn't need to be there and wanted to find out who."

"But what tipped him off to that? What did he see or hear to make him suspect that?"

Bryce gave a low groan. "He thought there might be some cops—or at least one—on a drug ring's payroll, but he didn't know who. He just had his suspicions and told me who he wanted me to ride with. He wanted to know if any of them made unauthorized stops or met with anyone suspicious. Honestly, I didn't know what exactly I was looking for, but Frank seemed to think I'd recognize it when I saw it—probably a phone call or a meeting that didn't look on the up and up. I don't know."

Tony caught her attention and motioned for her to follow him to the back. Bryce stayed on her heels and she let him. Once in his office, Tony jabbed a finger at her. "You've got to leave. You're going to get me killed."

Jade blinked. "What are you talking about?"

"Frank was making enemies left and right. And now you tell me he's disappeared. You two need to be smart and learn from that. Get out and don't come back here unless it's to shoot."

"Tony, if you're worried about—"

A shot rang out, and Jade and Bryce ducked as one. Glass from the shattered window hit the floor the same time as Tony, the blood stain on his chest growing bigger by the second. The second bullet whizzed past Jade's left ear, and she grabbed Bryce's arm as she threw herself behind the desk.

Bryce landed in an awkward heap next to Jade, thrown off balance by her frantic yank. She scrambled around him. "Are you okay?"

"Yeah. You?"

"Can you check on Tony and call 911 while I go after the shooter?"

She pulled her gun from her holster and, without waiting for an answer, headed for the office back door.

"Jade! Don't!"

Of course, she ignored him. Heart thundering, fighting his protective instincts that urged him to go after her and the need to help the wounded man, Bryce reminded himself that this was Jade's job and she was trained for this. Then again, so was he. Flashes from the past rose to haunt him, gunfire erupting in his mind while his buddies fell around him.

*Save them, have to save them!*

Bryce crawled over to Tony, ignoring the pull of memories he'd thought he'd dealt with. Bullets popping. Bombs exploding. He closed his eyes and clenched his teeth. *Help him!*

The man was conscious and his hand gripped Bryce's. "How bad is it?"

Bryce's eyes shot open, his mind cleared and training took over. "Not that bad. Hold on." Spotting a roll of unopened cleaning rags on the bottom shelf next to the desk, Bryce grabbed them and yanked out a handful. Turning, he pressed them to the wound in Tony's side. Keeping pressure on the area, Bryce dialed 911.

"911. What's your emergency?"

He rattled off the information as fast—and as clearly—as possible. "One man shot. Officer needs help. And I need an ambulance."

The sound of fingers clicking on the keyboard reached him. "One's on the way."

*God, please protect Jade and don't let Tony die.*

"Hang on, buddy," he said. "Help's coming."

"It's bad, isn't it?" Tony gasped.

"Naw, just a nick." Bryce fell back into combat zone mentality. *No matter how bad it is, don't say.* The roll of duct tape on the top shelf caught his attention. He took Tony's hand and pressed it over the wound. "Hold this and don't let go."

Tony's pain-filled gaze met his. "Come on, man. How bad? I...served, too."

"Yeah, well, this isn't the Middle East. You're going to be fine." He grabbed the tape and ripped strips, then pressed them over the rags. Tony hissed at the pressure. "You hear me? Help's on the way. You're going to be all right."

No response. He turned. Tony's dark eyelashes rested on waxen cheeks, and his chest rose with shallow breaths. Blood trickled from the side of his mouth. Bryce's tension amped higher. "Hold on, Tony," he whispered. "Please hold on."

*Incoming!* The explosion rocked him, but only in his mind. Sweat poured from him.

Bryce shook his head.

"Bryce!"

He turned to find Jade staring at him.

"You okay?" she asked.

How long had she been calling his name? He sucked in a breath. "Yeah. Fine. Where's backup and the paramedics?"

"Almost here. How's Tony?"

"He's unconscious, but still breathing."

Another long minute passed, but finally the sound of sirens reached him. Officers rushed in. As soon as they cleared the scene, paramedics hurried to Tony, and Bryce stepped back.

He turned to Jade, who studied him. "You sure you're all right?" she asked, her eyes clouded with concern.

"I'm fine. What have you got?"

She held up a bag. "Found the weapon. A witness saw him toss it into a trash can. Probably worried about getting caught with it. I'm going to get the registration number off this weapon and see if we can find out who it's registered to."

"If it's registered," Bryce said.

"True."

Bryce waited while Jade spoke to fellow officers and passed the weapon off to one of the crime scene unit members.

Two hours later, Bryce had finished giving his own statement and was now in the role of observer, trying to figure out his next move while he studied the cops on the scene. Not that the cops Frank suspected of being dirty would have it stamped on their forehead, but he wanted to remember faces. He would put names to them later.

Jade approached, looking tired and worried. "You okay?" he asked.

She kept asking him that and he wondered what he'd done to give away his internal struggle against the memories. "Sure. I'm fine."

"No, you're not."

"Yeah, I am. What about you?"

She arched a brow at him, and he knew he wasn't fooling her. "Ready to go home," she said. "I can do the paperwork on this from there."

"I'll follow you," he said.

"No need. I have to stop and get a Christmas tree before I walk through the door or my name will be mud."

"I'll still go with you."

She didn't move, just studied him, a new look in her eyes. A guarded one that he didn't like. Before he could wonder about the source of it, she shook her head.

"What am I missing, Bryce?"

"What do you mean?"

"Who was the target? Tony? Or me? Us? I don't think it's a coincidence that Tony got shot the morning I came to talk to him."

"I agree." He paused. "Did someone follow you here?"

"Possibly. Or you." She rubbed her head as her phone

buzzed. "Detective Hollis. Uh-huh. Okay, thanks. That's kind of what I figured." When she hung up, Bryce raised a brow. "The weapon I recovered was stolen."

"Of course it was."

"Yeah."

"So, what now? Home or…?" He let his sentence trail off, hoping she'd fill in the blank.

"Now we check with Heather and see if she's heard anything from any of Frank's friends on our way to the hospital to check on Tony Swift." She cut her eyes to Bryce. "He knows way more than he was telling us. Then I find a Christmas tree and go home to decorate it with my—um—the kids."

"How many kids are staying with your parents right now?"

"Just…well, three."

"It's crazy to think how many kids have come and gone over the years. They're really special people."

"I know." She paused. "They're talking about adopting the twins in their care right now."

"Oh. Really?"

"Yes."

"Wow." He cleared his throat. "That's a lot of responsibility."

Her eyes went frosty. "No kidding. I'll be sure to pass that tip on to them."

"I didn't mean—"

"Some of us don't run away from responsibility. Some of us actually embrace it."

He blinked at the hostility shimmering in her voice. "Hey, Jade, I didn't mean anything—"

"Don't worry about it. Are you ready to head to the hospital?"

He stared at her for a moment before shrugging. "Um…sure."

"Great. You can follow me if that's all right with you." She didn't bother to wait for his agreement but headed for her vehicle.

Bryce frowned. He'd really struck a nerve with Jade. Her reaction seemed to indicate that he ran from responsibility, but what would give her that idea? The fact that he'd stayed the night—that one night—and never contacted her? Probably. She knew he was leaving and why, but she had no idea why he'd stayed away from home for six years with minimal contact. And zero contact with *her*. Could that be interpreted as running from responsibility somehow? Maybe. Again, probably. At least in her eyes.

He started to ask her, but her hard jaw and narrowed eyes said right now might not be the best time to broach the subject. He had a feeling if Jade chose to let loose the words she'd swallowed, they might be more deadly than the bullets that had been fired at him earlier that day.

A good soldier knew when to attack and when to retreat.

And Bryce had been a very good soldier.

# FIVE

Captain Colson called just as Jade pulled into one of the hospital parking spots reserved for police. She tapped the screen and lifted the phone to her ear. "Hi, Captain."

"Jade, how are you doing?"

"Hanging in there, sir, thanks."

"I got your message about needing a warrant to pull security footage from the cameras across the street from the range. That's set in motion and I'll be in touch as soon as I hear something. You can come in and take a look at it if you like. See if anything stands out."

Bryce approached the passenger side, and she motioned for him to get in while she was on the phone.

"Thank you, sir." She paused.

"Something else on your mind?"

"Yes. I think..." Another pause.

"Say what you need to say, Jade."

"I think we should get a cadaver dog out to the mill where we found the shirt." The words rushed from her mouth, and Bryce's head whipped around to stare at her. She bit her lip and looked away from him.

Captain Colson grunted. "All right. I'll get one out there."

"Thanks." She hung up and shot a look at Bryce. The

tight set of his jaw said he wanted to protest and was keeping his tongue in line with great effort. "I just want to rule it out."

"I know."

"His shirt was found there with two bullet holes in it. I just can't get that out of my mind."

"I know, Jade."

While the warrant and the dog were being taken care of, she wanted to check on Tony. She still wasn't convinced he didn't know something about Frank's whereabouts, and if he was awake, he might be more inclined to talk now that he'd been shot.

"You ready to see if Tony is awake?"

"I'll follow you." She climbed out of the SUV and walked into the hospital.

Bryce stayed right behind her. She shouldn't have been so curt with him about the whole responsibility thing. Just because he wasn't ready—or didn't want—to have kids didn't mean he wasn't responsible. It just meant he wasn't ready—or he simply didn't want kids. He had his reasons, and she needed to respect that even if she didn't like it.

She was being too antsy, letting her emotions get the best of her. But that scene at the shooting range had gotten to her. He'd been in the middle of a PTSD attack if she'd ever seen one. And she had. The guy she'd dated for a while in Charlotte had had severe PTSD attacks and had refused to deal with them. Much like Bryce had just done. He'd brushed it off and she'd had to let him for now, but she planned to address it at some point. She had to if he was ever going to be a part of Mia's life—assuming he wanted to be. Regardless, once she told him about Mia, there'd be no going back, and it wasn't a decision that was black and white anymore.

Added to the stress of the day, Heather hadn't answered her calls or acknowledged the voice mails Jade had left, so they knew no more than they had thirty minutes ago about Frank's timeline and who the last person to see him might have been.

Jade flashed her badge at the woman sitting at the desk in the surgery waiting room. Her name tag read Martha Bolton. "Hi, Ms. Bolton, I'm Detective Hollis. You had a patient brought in a few hours ago. Tony Swift. I need to talk to him when he wakes up. Do you know how long that might be?"

The woman consulted her computer and frowned. "He's still in surgery, so I'd say you might have a pretty long wait."

Of course. "Have any of his family arrived?"

"I believe his wife." She nodded to the corner, where a woman in her midthirties twisted a tissue between her fingers.

"Thank you. I may have to leave after I talk to her, but if I give you my card, would you call and let me know when he's out?"

"Of course, I'll be happy to." Mrs. Bolton took the card and taped it to the monitor of her computer.

"So, we talk to Tony's wife?" Bryce asked.

"*I* talk to Tony's wife. You can have a seat and wait for me to finish."

He pursed his lips. "Come on, Jade, Frank's my friend, too."

She sighed. "Fine, but let me do the talking, please?"

"Sure."

Jade walked over to stand in front of the woman. "Mrs. Swift?"

She looked up. "Yes?"

"I'm Jade Hollis. We met last night—or early this morning, rather."

"I remember. You came looking for Tony." Her eyes flashed. "So, it's your fault he got shot?"

"No, ma'am. I place that blame on the shooter."

"Why were you looking for him? He refused to tell me."

"Do you know a man by the name of Frank Shipman?"

She frowned. "Sounds familiar, but I can't place him."

Bryce pulled out his phone, tapped the screen, then turned it so the woman could see it. "That's him. The woman on his left is his fiancée."

Mrs. Swift studied the photo while she continued to shred the tissue, not seeming to notice—or care—that she was making a pile of white on the floor between her feet. "I think I've seen him before."

"Where?"

"At the diner. He and Tony were having coffee one morning. I clean the bank across the street and I'd locked my keys in the car. When I called Tony, he told me he was at the diner, so I walked over there to get Tony's keys."

"And Tony didn't say why they were meeting?"

She shook her head. "But I got the feeling he wasn't happy with your friend. As I was walking out, I heard him say something like, 'Stay out of things that don't concern you. It could be dangerous for your health.'"

Jade shot a glance at Bryce. "That's basically what he told us this morning right before the shooting."

"Which means he got shot because you were nosing around."

"Again, no. If he got shot, it was because he was

involved in something he shouldn't have been." She paused. "If he was the target."

"Mrs. Swift?"

Jade turned at the new voice to find a woman in scrubs and a surgical cap standing behind them.

Tony's wife stood. "Yes. Is he okay?"

"I'm Dr. Grey. It was touch and go for a while there, but right now your husband's stable. He'll be in the ICU for tonight at least. I'm not going to sugarcoat it. A scant inch more to the left and that bullet would have hit his heart."

She gasped and paled. Jade placed a hand on her arm. "But it didn't."

"No, it didn't. You're right. Should he make it through the night, he'll have a long road to recovery ahead of him."

Mrs. Swift nodded. "Thank you."

"Someone will be out to let you know when you can come back to see him."

The doctor left, and Jade turned back to the woman. "Can you think of anything else? Any other connection between your husband and Frank Shipman."

"No. Nothing."

"If you think of anything, will you call?" Jade held out her card.

Mrs. Swift took it. "Yeah, sure. Excuse me." She walked toward the restrooms, and Bryce turned to Jade.

"Now what?" he asked.

"I'm not quite ready to leave yet. Do you mind if we go down to the cafeteria and talk for a bit? I've got some questions for you."

He followed her down to the restaurant, where she ordered a coffee. Bryce did the same and they found a table.

Jade took a sip and tried to find the words that had been burning a hole in her tongue ever since she'd seen Bryce in the old mill. But first… "I shouldn't have jumped on you about the whole responsibility thing. I'm sorry." She drew in a deep breath. "If having children isn't something you want to do, then I shouldn't make digs about it." And she shouldn't, but trying to tell him about Mia was wearing on her. However, she needed to know more about his feelings in order to see if there was a chance that he might change his mind. She'd feel much better about revealing his status as Mia's father if he was even on the fence about having children. But if he stayed adamantly opposed… "Tell me why you don't want kids, Bryce. I don't think I've ever actually asked." A pang of remorse hit her. She'd just assumed that he didn't want them interfering with his life plans. But maybe it was more than that.

"Mostly because of my parents. My father in particular. He's so controlling and cold. I never felt like he loved me—or Kristy." He swallowed and looked away. "It was almost like he *couldn't*. And I just… I just… I can't take a chance on being the same way with a child of my own."

"I remember how he was. I guess I just don't understand what makes you think you'd be anything like that when you don't have one ounce of his temperament." She paused. "And Kristy doesn't seem to have any issues when it comes to loving her children."

He rubbed a hand over his head. "Trust me, I've noticed that. Now, what other questions do you have for me?"

Jade frowned and debated whether she wanted to drop it. Finally, she decided it wouldn't accomplish anything. And besides, she had other answers she wanted. "I know we already talked about this a little bit, but can you just clarify why you didn't call me? Me. Specifically me. I thought we were friends. I thought we would at least keep in touch, but…" She spread her hands at a loss for words.

He looked up and sighed. "I didn't call anyone, Jade. I was in a bad place for a long time after the explosion."

"Tell me about it."

"I…it was…hard. Three months into serving, our convoy was hit with an IED. I had a long recovery. Surgery, physical therapy and more. I just couldn't cope with it all, I guess, so I traveled."

"Traveled? Where'd you go?"

"Anywhere the bus went. I saw a lot of the Middle East, Europe, and even made my way to South America at one point."

"But you talked to Frank, right?"

"Every so often. He was my link to this other life that I felt no longer existed for me."

She gaped. "No longer existed?"

Another sigh. "You have to understand. I was dealing with a lot."

"And that prevented you from picking up a phone?"

He shut his eyes for a moment. "Yes. It did."

Jade didn't know what to say or how to react, so she sipped her coffee. Coffee she no longer wanted. *Say it. Tell him.* "Bryce, there's something you… I need to say… You have…" She stopped. "I told Frank to ask you to call me. Why didn't you?"

His gaze locked on hers. "What?"

"I told him I needed you to call me. That's why I'm so…well, angry." And hurt.

Bryce frowned. "Frank never told me to call you."

She gaped. "I told him several times. And each time he promised he would—and had. When I asked him why I hadn't heard from you, he always gave me a pretty good answer why you hadn't called. Why would he lie about that?"

Bryce shook his head. "I have no idea, unless…"

"What?"

"Unless he thought he was protecting me in some way."

"Protecting you? From what?"

He raked a hand over his buzz cut. "From stress. Added pressure. From… I don't know." He paused, looked away. "I thought you'd hate me after that night. Your grandmother had just died and you were grieving. You looked to me for comfort and I…" He trailed off, swallowed and met her gaze once more.

"You didn't take advantage, Bryce. We're both responsible for that night." And she really didn't want to talk about that.

He seemed to sense her discomfort. "Why did you want me to call you?"

"I… It's… I'm… Because…" She stopped. Why oh why couldn't she simply say the words? But no, this wasn't the place to blurt it out. Her mind was still spinning that Frank hadn't passed on her request for Bryce to call her. "I think it's time to get out of here."

Confusion pulled his brows together. "What is it?"

"Nothing. At least right now. I can't think straight. Come on, please. We need to see if Heather's heard anything from Frank."

"She would have called if she'd heard anything." He dropped his gaze to the cup in his right hand. "I have a bad feeling about him, Jade," he said softly. "And I don't like or want that feeling."

She blew out a low breath and blinked back a sudden surge of tears. "I know. I have the same feeling."

He looked up. "I want to believe he's alive."

"Well, he's not dead until…we discover differently. That's why I wanted the cadaver dog out there." She pressed fingers to her tired eyes, then dropped her hands. "Ready?"

"Ready for you to tell me whatever it is you're finding so hard to spit out."

She flinched. "This isn't the time or the place."

He studied her for a moment, then nodded. "All right. I can wait. What now?"

"It's getting close to five o'clock, and I still need to buy a Christmas tree and take it home while we wait to hear from Heather or…someone who's seen Frank."

"Then let's go."

Bryce rode in silence while Jade drove to a Christmas tree lot on the outskirts of town. He absently watched the sun sink behind the horizon while he tried to sort through the fact that Frank hadn't told him Jade was trying to get in touch with him. He couldn't fathom that, but he also didn't see Jade lying about it. She'd been honestly perplexed and angry. And definitely hurt.

Unless he was right in his thinking that Frank thought he was protecting Bryce in some way, it made no sense that his friend wouldn't have passed on Jade's messages to call her.

But the whole protection angle didn't sit right with him. He shook his head, wishing he could just ask Frank what he'd been thinking.

And why had Jade wanted him to call her anyway? He'd figured she'd never want to see or talk to him again after that night. Maybe he should just ask her like he wished he could ask Frank.

He slid a glance at her and noted her slim but strong hands on the wheel, the confident way she drove and the frown pulling her brows to the bridge of her nose. Instead of broaching subjects that made them both uncomfortable, he took the safe route. "How are you going to tie a tree on top of this SUV? Do you have some cables in here?"

"I do." She shot him a sideways glance. "Which is where you come in since you have the honor of accompanying me." Her tone was light, teasing, but her gaze was serious as it went to the side mirror, then the rearview one.

"Where I come in? How do you figure?"

"I'm going to let you help get it up there." Once again, she checked the mirrors. He did the same and noted traffic, but nothing that warranted her vigilance.

"Oh." He tried to figure out how he would do that with one good leg. In his mind, he pictured the process and thought he might be able to do it without looking like an idiot.

"What is it?" she asked.

"Nothing. The kids didn't want to pick the tree out themselves?"

She laughed. A real laugh that shot straight to his heart. "I asked them that, but they said no, it was too cold and they'd be content with just decorating it."

"Huh. Those sound like some interesting kids you've got living with you."

"Ha, you're telling me." He caught her sideways glance. She opened her mouth, then shut it, did another mirror check and frowned.

"What is it?" he asked.

"Just being careful."

"You see something I need to be concerned about?"

She looked again. "Not right now."

"Okay, then what were you going to say just a minute ago?"

Jade shrugged. "I was thinking about asking if you'd like to come help decorate it, but it would entail hanging out with the children."

He sighed. "I don't dislike children as long as they belong to other people. And I'd love to come help decorate if I can bring my dog."

"You have a dog?"

"I do, but don't worry. She's well trained and great with kids."

"Then both of you are welcome to come," she said, pulling into the lot. "Assuming we find a tree under all that snow."

"We'll find one."

She got out of the SUV and pulled on her gloves and hat. Bryce slammed the passenger door shut and rounded the front of the vehicle, noting the rows and rows of trees. The sun had completely set, blanketing the area in darkness, but the lights strung from post to post created a festive air of anticipation. A gust of wind whipped around her and she shivered. "I think I'd like to make this a quick shopping trip," she said.

"I'm with you." He pulled the collar of his coat tighter around his neck and slipped his gloves on.

"Howdy folks." An older man in his early seventies who looked immune to the cold approached. His thick red-and-black-plaid hat was pulled low over his ears, and he had the matching Sherpa-lined coat buttoned to his chin. "I'm Clay Foster. Let me know when you find what you need. I'm a little short on workers tonight, but that doesn't seem to matter." He looked around. "Not many people want to get out in this." He clasped his gloved hands together, then rubbed them. "Shorter trees are to the left. Taller to the right. When you find the one you want, just let me know. I'll be in the office in front of the heater."

"Thank you, sir," Jade said.

He nodded and wandered back to the fifth wheel he'd called his office.

Bryce looked around. "This place is huge. You could get lost in here."

"Maybe once we're in the middle of the trees, they'll shield us from the wind."

"Good idea." It helped, but not much. Bryce followed her from one tree to the next, noting she looked at her phone every few minutes. "Nothing about Frank, huh?"

"No."

"I don't know whether that's good or bad?"

"Both," she muttered.

Good in that they hadn't discovered a body. Bad in that no one had found Frank. Her phone rang, and she swiped the screen. "Heather? Are you okay?" She listened for a moment, then nodded at Bryce. "I understand. Yeah. And nothing? Right. Thanks. Stay in touch."

"What'd she say?"

"That she hadn't heard from Frank, but that she learned he'd stopped by their church yesterday around lunchtime, asking to talk to the pastor who was going to marry them."

"About what?"

"She didn't know and neither did the pastor—which is where she's been. She turned her ringer off to talk to him and didn't notice my call until just now. Anyway, the pastor wasn't there when Frank dropped in so the church secretary, Donna, scheduled an appointment for tomorrow at ten in the morning."

"Wedding ceremony questions or something else?" Bryce muttered.

"No one but Frank knows that right now, but at least we know where he was later in the day after you talked to him."

A particularly hard gust of wind broke through the line of trees, and Bryce shuddered. He was freezing. And he didn't want to admit it, but his leg was killing him. He started to say something and noticed her attention to a particular tree. "That one?"

"Yes. This one. It's perfect." She checked the price and grimaced but waved to Clay. He nodded he'd be there in a minute, and Bryce breathed a sigh of relief. The tree wasn't that big and shouldn't be too hard to handle even with his damaged leg. She rubbed her temple, and he noted the strain around her mouth along with the tight jaw.

"Head hurting?"

"Yes. I think I need to take more ibuprofen."

"Y'all need help?"

Bryce nodded to the worker. "That'd be great."

"I'll pay while you guys get the tree taken care of, if that's all right," Jade said.

"Great," Bryce said. At least if he fumbled the tree, she wouldn't be around to witness it.

He looked at Clay. "Ready?"

"Let's do it."

Jade headed for the office, pulling her wallet from her purse and doing her best to ignore the increased pounding in her head. Pounding caused by more than her physical injury. His words continued to echo even as she tried to plan to tell him about Mia—which was part of the reason she wanted to invite him to help with the tree. He didn't mind children *as long as they belonged to other people.*

Would she be doing the right thing in telling him about Mia when he clearly wasn't interested in being a father? Would the knowledge do more harm than good? Just because he *deserved* to know didn't mean it was the best thing for him to actually know.

Her main concern was what was best for Mia. She had to put her first. But she should at least introduce Bryce to Mia so she could see them together and *then* make a decision about telling him. She groaned. What an absolutely horrid plan.

A crunch of a footstep on snow from behind her brought her to a halt, and she turned. The snow-covered path was empty. For a moment, she stood there, examining the area. Only the row of trees greeted her, and the shiver that swept through her had nothing to do with the cold. After the attack at the mill, then the shooting at the range, she was jumpy.

Jade picked up the pace and wished the office wasn't so far away. She replaced her wallet and slung the purse over shoulder, then removed the glove from her right hand. She glanced around once more, noting the empty area. It was late, and most families who'd visited had done so during the daylight hours. Clay had been right. Not many people wanted to get out in this weather, not to mention the dark. She reached for the weapon that rested in her shoulder holster.

Just as her fingers curled over it, the lights flickered, then went out. Darkness covered her. A rush of footsteps pounded behind her. As she turned, she pulled her weapon, and something wrapped around her throat. Squeezing. Warm breath panted against her right ear.

Panic flared. Her gun tumbled from her fingers and

she grasped at the cord around her neck. With no time to scream, her only thought was she didn't want to die like this. Jade kicked back and connected with a shin. The person gasped and let out a low grunt. For a moment, she could breathe and managed to shove a hand up under the cable milliseconds before it drew tight again. Her frantic brain registered rubber. Not wire.

Adrenaline racing, she curled her fingers around the vise and pulled, but the person behind her was strong and using Jade's own hand to press against her throat to cut off her air. A squeak escaped from her and she jabbed back with her opposite elbow, despairing when she hit nothing. Stars started to dance in front of her eyes. *Please God! I don't want to leave the children. Please!*

"Jade!"

*Bryce!*

"Hey, Jade! Where are you?"

Then she was free. She sank to her knees, gasping, dragging in deep breaths of cold air. She scrambled to her feet, hand searching for her weapon. Her fingers brushed over it, and she snagged it as a light bounced off the ground and into her face. She held up a hand to block the glare and spun to look in the direction the person had gone, but the darkness was complete. Dizziness hit her and she sank to the ground once more, coughing.

"Jade, what happened?" Bryce was there, hands on her shoulders.

"Attacked," she wheezed. Her throat ached, but at least she could breathe. He grabbed whatever it was the attacker had wrapped around her throat and tugged it away.

"What in the world?" She recognized Clay's voice. He ran toward her, the beam of the flashlight bouncing along the muddy snow. "What happened? Are you okay?" he asked when he reached her.

Bryce told him in clipped sentences what had happened.

"I'm so sorry."

"Call an ambulance," Bryce said, running his hands up and down her arms, then tilting her head to examine her throat.

"No, don't need an ambulance. It's okay," Jade said. "It's getting better." She heard the harsh rasp in her voice and understood Bryce's doubtful look.

"If you don't need me," Clay said, "I'm going to see if I can get the lights back on."

"Yeah, that would be good." Bryce turned back to Jade. "You could have serious damage to your throat." The mixture of terror and fury in his words stilled her. Touched her.

"Possibly," she croaked, "but I don't think so. I managed to get my hand up there and pull against it, minimizing the harm." She hoped. "Man, that was scary." Tears gathered and she shoved them away, coughing once more. "I just want to go home and crawl into bed." The minute the words left her mouth, she wished she could haul them back in. She sounded helpless and weak. But she'd just been attacked, so maybe she should cut herself a break.

"Come on," Bryce said, "I'll help you to the car."

"I've got to write all this up."

"Then I'll wait on you."

She narrowed her eyes. "I don't remember you being this bossy."

He huffed a laugh that did nothing to erase the worry in his eyes. "It's not bossy, it's common sense."

The lights came on and she blinked against the sudden

brightness—and recognized her attacker's weapon. "I was almost strangled with a strand of Christmas lights? You've got to be kidding." She gave a humorless bark of laughter that sent pain racing through her throat. She immediately cut it short and coughed once more.

"Jade, I really think you should see someone."

"No. I just need to get some ice on it, take some more ibuprofen, and rest."

"So stubborn."

"Exactly. So, let's go," she whispered, unable to speak any louder at this point.

With Bryce's help, she stood, gathered her purse and started walking toward the office. She noted him favoring his left leg, but before she could ask him about it, Clay spotted them and hurried toward them. "Are you sure you're okay, ma'am? I went ahead and called the cops to report it, but I can still call an ambulance."

"I'll be sore for a while, but I'm all right, I think. Thank you." What was one more sore place on her already bruised and battered body?

"Well, it's not much, but the tree is on us. And your friend can come back and get one, too."

"That's very kind of you, thank you."

Three police cruisers pulled into the parking lot. She recognized Dylan. Abby Jones climbed out of the second car, and Tom Williams bolted from the third.

"Jade!" Abby rushed toward her. "You okay?"

"I'm alive. That probably wasn't on the agenda for my attacker. The strand of lights is back there. Can you bag it and see if there are any prints other than mine and Bryce's on there?"

"Of course. What happened?"

Her head pounded and her throat hurt. She seriously didn't want to deal with this tonight.

"Save your voice," Bryce said. He gave the woman the short version.

"I'll sit in my vehicle and write up the report," Jade whispered. "It won't take me long." A thought hit her. She turned to Clay. "Do you have a closed-circuit television? Security footage?"

"Absolutely, but I'm not sure how much you'll be able to see in the dark."

Jade nodded, then wished she hadn't. She pressed a hand to her head. "We'll want to try anyway. See if it picked up anything before the lights went out. Abby, can you get a copy of it so we can take a look at who was around?"

"Of course."

"Thanks."

Bryce joined her while she worked on the report. When she was done, she hit Send. "Nice job on strapping the tree down."

"The credit goes mostly to Clay, but thanks." He reached for her hand, then lightly touched her throat. "That was scary, Jade," he whispered.

She swallowed, and his eyes followed the movement, then lifted to her eyes. She cleared her throat and grimaced. "Yeah, it was. But I'm okay."

"But you were hurt once again." His hand lifted to cup her chin. "I don't handle it well when you get hurt."

The look in his eyes had changed. While caring and concern were still there, something else had crept in. A warmth and awareness she'd not seen quite as strong before. "I...well... I don't know what to say to that."

"It's okay. I'm not exactly sure how to explain it."

"Okay then." She glanced away then back. "I noticed you were limping. Are you all right?"

A small smile flickered, then faded, and she let out a

small relieved breath when he dropped his hand from her cheek to lean back. "I've just been on my leg too long. As soon as I get off of it, I'll be all right."

She raised a brow, finally able to breathe now that he'd put some space between them. "What's wrong with your leg?"

He shot her a funny look. "Kristy didn't tell you?"

"Tell me what?"

"I lost the lower part of my left leg in that IED blast. I have a prosthetic."

She gaped. Then snapped her mouth shut. "I had no idea. You can't tell. Frank didn't say anything about it, either." Frank hadn't said much of anything, apparently. "I'm so sorry. I'm...wow."

He shrugged. "It took me a while to come to grips with it, but I have a buddy who lost an arm, and he's been a big help."

"I'm glad." Very glad. The more insights into his life over the past six years that he revealed, the more her long-held anger started to fade.

"So, are we ready to do this?" he asked.

She studied him a moment longer, then nodded, wincing slightly. "Sure, but I'm hoping I can convince the kids to put off decorating the tree until tomorrow night." It was a wimpy way to end the day, but her body was done.

"I understand. I'll help you get it in the house, and Sasha and I'll join you tomorrow, if that's all right."

"Sounds perfect."

Her phone rang, and she activated the vehicle's Bluetooth to answer it. "Hi, Captain. Just to let you know, I'm driving and you're on Speaker. Bryce Kingsley is with me."

"Got it. First, how are you doing? Are you all right? You've sure been having a tough couple of days."

"It's been rough for sure. I'm heading home now."

"Take some time off. You need to heal. I've got two of our best detectives on this, so you can rest easy. I've also told them to keep you updated on anything they find out."

Bryce kept his mouth shut at the words but nodded his agreement and made sure she saw him do it. She rolled her eyes at him. "Captain, can we just see how I feel in the morning? I'm not ready to quit looking for Frank just yet."

"That's up to you. I did want to let you know that I've got the shooting range security footage."

"That's good news."

"I know you wanted to look at it, but in light of this recent attack on you, don't worry about it for now. I'll watch it and let you know what we find out—if anything."

"I can come in and watch—"

"Hold on a second. Got a call coming in from the cadaver dog handler."

Jade's breath lodged in her throat. She drove in silence, every nerve on alert. Bryce had stilled, his only movement to curl his fingers into fists.

Two minutes later, the captain came back on the line. "You there?"

"Yes, sir."

"Jade, I..."

"Sir? Just say it, please."

"I hate it, but they've found a body out in the woods behind the mill," he said, his voice rough with compassion. "According to the wallet next to the body, it's Frank Shipman."

# SIX

Bryce's whole body went still. A tear tracked down Jade's cheek and she sniffed.

"Jade?" The captain's voice broke through the shock.

"Yes, sir," she said. "Give me a moment to regroup and I'll be right there."

"You don't—" Captain Colson sighed. "Of course you'll go. I understand. Be careful."

"Of course."

"I'm so sorry, Jade. I was really hoping for a different outcome."

"Thank you, sir. We all were." She hung up, pulled into a grocery store parking lot and put the vehicle in Park.

A sob slipped out. Bryce reached for her, and she gripped his hand then leaned her head against the steering wheel to cry. Her grief mingled with his, and he settled his head back against the seat, closed his eyes, and tried to keep his composure even though his heartbeat pounded in his ears. *Not Frank. Please not Frank.* But if he'd learned anything from his bout of depression, denial didn't work.

*God, why Frank?*

"How am I going to tell Heather?" Jade whispered. She touched her throat and grimaced.

"Sore?"

She nodded. "Hurts worse when I cry." She sniffed and swiped her eyes. "I need to call my mom. The kids will be so disappointed about putting off the tree again, but it can't be helped."

"They'll understand when you explain."

"Yes. At least, I hope so." With another squeeze to his hand, she released him. He wanted to grab her hand back and tell her not to make the call just yet, but he kept silent. The first call to her mother didn't take long. He heard the woman's sharp cry, and more tears squeezed out from Jade's closed eyes. After she hung up, she grabbed several tissues from the center console and wiped her face. "The captain said his wallet was on him. That's why they believe it's him."

"Doesn't mean someone couldn't have stolen it and gotten killed and buried with it."

She shot him a sidelong glance and he sighed, pressed his fingers to his eyes and swallowed hard. "I know, I know. Not likely. Are you up to driving?"

Jade nodded. "Guess I have to be. You can't drive my vehicle." She pulled a bottle of ibuprofen out of the glove compartment and popped four.

He held out a hand, and she gave him the bottle. He took four, too, replaced the cap and returned it to the compartment. "All right, then."

"All right, then," she echoed.

Ten minutes later found them on an active scene. Floodlights had been set up, and the medical examiner was on site. Bryce limped behind Jade as she ducked under the tape and flashed her badge. She signed the crime scene log and motioned for him to follow her.

His eyes landed on the medical examiner, who was bent over a body.

Jade stopped, and Bryce heard her breath hitch. He gripped her elbow, not sure if it was to comfort her or steady himself. Maybe both.

"Hi, Neal," Jade said to the medical examiner as she pulled the scarf tighter around her neck. He figured she was hiding the marks left by her attacker more than trying to block out the cold.

Neal nodded. "Jade."

"Is it Frank?"

The man stepped back to give them a better view, and Bryce shuddered.

"Yeah," she whispered. "It's him."

"You were friends?"

She nodded, and Bryce looked away.

"Can you tell the cause of death?" she asked.

"Not at the moment."

"Lift his shirt up, will you?" she said. "Please?"

Neal raised a brow, but did as Jade requested. His eyes went wide and jerked back to Jade. "Whoa. I guess we know what killed him."

Two bullet holes in his chest, and Bryce had no doubt they'd line up with the jersey they'd found.

"Someone changed his shirt?" Neal asked.

"Yes."

"But why?"

"When I find his killer, I'll be sure to ask," Jade said. Her voice had gone cold with determination. "I guess we have to tell Heather and his family now."

Bryce grimaced, and dread filled him. Frank's sister, Lisa, would be devastated. And Heather—

His hands curled into fists and he forced himself to

breathe slow, even breaths as his heart thundered in his chest with grief—and the need to *do* something.

He waited and watched as Jade spoke to the officers. Finally, she joined him while they loaded Frank's body into the black bag and placed him in the back of the coroner's red Yukon.

"Frank!"

He spun to see Heather slam her car door and race toward them.

Bryce stepped forward and caught her before she could pass him.

"Heather, stop."

"I heard it on the police scanner. Is it him?"

"Yes, it's him. I'm so sorry."

"No!" Sobs ripped from her and he felt her knees give out. Holding her nearly rocked him off balance, but then Jade was there, taking her friend and partner into her arms and lowering her to the ground—an action that Bryce would have found very difficult to do. Gratitude and resentment shot through him. He tried to focus on the first and ignore the second. The woman had just lost her fiancé. He and Jade had just lost a friend. Now wasn't the time to let self-pity rear its head.

"I'm so sorry, Heather," he said. "So very sorry." Jade's dark eyes met his, and his heart lurched at the agony reflected there. "We'll find who did this," he said. "We will."

Heather didn't seem to hear him, but Jade nodded. "Yes, oh, yes, we will."

In the back of her cruiser, Jade held Heather while her friend cried, then helped her get herself together. Heather took two deep breaths and let them out slowly. "I want to go with him to the morgue."

Jade didn't even bother to try to talk her out of it. "I'll ride with you."

"There's no reason for you to. You need to go home."

"Right. Like I'd leave you. The kids have my parents there." She paused. "Should I call your mom?"

Heather's parents had divorced when she and Jade were still teens, but Heather was very close to her mother—or at least she had been, up until she'd ignored the woman's warnings about marrying the man who'd wound up leaving her at the altar. "We haven't talked in forever, but she was happy for me. Glad I'd found Frank and was over the jerk."

"Of course she was." Heather had told her all of this months ago. "You want me to call her?"

"I'll do it." She hiccupped but made no move to reach for her phone. "I don't want to go home," she whispered. "I can't."

"I understand. I'll go by your house and pack a bag for you."

"No!"

Jade jerked. "Okay."

Heather sighed and rubbed her eyes. "I'm sorry. I didn't mean to yell. It's just that all of those clothes... Ugh. Frank and I went shopping a lot. He bought me a lot of them and every single stitch will remind me of him. I think I'll go to a hotel and tell Mom to bring me something to wear for now. I have a few outfits at her house."

"Okay, whatever you want to do."

"That's what I want."

Two hours later, Jade stepped inside her home and shut the door behind her with a heavy sigh while biting back the tears that wanted to flow. Crying wouldn't bring Frank back—nor find his killer. And it simply hurt her throat too much to cry anymore. The kitchen night-light was on and the house smelled like fresh chocolate chip cookies. Bless her mother. She snagged a cookie from the plate someone had thoughtfully set on the foyer table and took a bite. She kicked off her shoes and pulled her weapon from her holster, checked to make sure the safety was engaged, then locked it in the box next to the cookies.

"Hi, Mommy." Jade looked up to find Mia lying on the couch, blanket pulled to her chin. "I'm sorry about your friend."

"Little bear, what are you doing up so late?"

"She couldn't sleep," Jade's father said from the kitchen door. "She kept waking Jessica up, so I brought her over here."

"Couldn't sleep? Why not?"

Mia patted the couch, and Jade understood that she was to sit next to her daughter. "Lolly told me about your friend. I was sad for you."

In spite of her resolution not to cry, Jade's throat tightened once more, and she slid her arm around her child to pull her snug against her side. Mia rested her head on Jade's shoulder. "Thank you," Jade said. "I'm sad, too. And I'm sorry I broke my promise to decorate the tree tonight."

"It's okay. We can do it tomorrow."

"You're the best, kiddo."

"I know."

Jade almost smiled at the child's uncomplicated self-esteem. "But you need to go to bed."

"I don't have school tomorrow, you know."

"That's a good thing, because you'd fall asleep and bruise your head on your math book."

"We don't have math books, silly. We have papers." Mia yawned. "Jessica's mad at you, though."

"Why? Because of the Christmas tree?"

"Uh-huh."

"I'll talk to Jessica. She'll be all right."

"'Kay."

The girl was almost asleep, her little body relaxing into Jade's with each passing second. With effort, ignoring her aches and pains, Jade carried Mia to her room and tucked her in with a kiss to her forehead. Then she sighed.

She hated breaking her promise. Most days she was home when she said she was going to be, but every once in a while she had days like today, and it meant changing or postponing plans. Mia had learned to roll with it, but Jessica and Gage hadn't. If her parents wound up adopting them, they'd learn their big sister sometimes had to change plans. It was disappointing, but not the end of the world. Still, with their background, it might seem like she was just another adult not to be trusted. What a fine line to have to walk.

Back in her small den area, she found her dad scrolling on his phone. He was a handsome man in his midfifties. And while his hair had turned gray around his ears and he had a few wrinkles around his eyes, he still looked much like he had when he'd walked down the aisle with Jade's mother thirty years ago. He glanced up when she entered and tucked his phone into his pocket. "I'm sorry about Frank, hon."

"Thank you. Me too." She rubbed the back of her neck with a groan. "It's been a very long day."

He walked over to massage her shoulders. "You're wound up tighter than a spring, kiddo."

"I'm sure." She dropped her chin to her chest. "Mia mentioned my friend. Mom didn't tell the kids who it was?"

"No." He dropped his hands. "Just that you had a friend who was hurt and had to go help."

"I see." She rubbed her eyes. She'd have to tell them. They knew and loved Frank and would wonder why he wasn't coming around anymore.

"Heather didn't want to come stay with you?" he asked. "With us?"

"No. I tried to get her to come and even told her I'd stay at her place, but she said she was going to stay with her mother tonight, and then at Frank's house—what was supposed to be *their* house—after the crime scene people do their thing and release it. She said she needed to be with her mom, to process and grieve." Jade bit her lip and shook her head. "I don't understand it. I talked to Frank on a weekly basis, sometimes more, and I never knew he was doing something this dangerous."

"Probably didn't tell you because he was afraid you'd tell Heather."

"Maybe." She shook her head. "He took Mia and the twins to his niece's birthday party two weeks ago. Were they in danger when they were with him? Would he have risked that?"

Her father took her hands. "No, honey, you know Frank. He wouldn't have put those kids in danger. Not knowingly."

She pulled away from him and looked at the ceiling as though she might find the answers written there.

A gasp pulled her gaze back to her father. He was staring at her throat. "What happened to you?"

She touched the area with a grimace. "I got caught in a strand of lights."

His eyes narrowed. "Caught how?"

"I… Someone at the tree lot attacked me and wrapped a strand of lights around my throat."

He blanched and his face paled. "Jade," he whispered. "Did they catch him?"

"No. Not yet. We're hoping to get some footage from the security cameras there."

He shook his head. "You've had too many life-threatening things happen lately, from getting attacked at the mill to the shooting at the range. Now this? It's too much."

"No kidding."

He paused. "Take a shower and go to bed. I'll stay here tonight."

"We have officers watching the place, Dad. We'll be okay."

"Are you willing to risk Mia's life on that? Yours?"

She hesitated. Then sighed. "I'll get you some blankets and a pillow."

"And I'm going to get my gun."

Bryce climbed the stairs to his room with Sasha on his heels. She'd missed him and now didn't want to leave his side. In his bathroom, with Sasha lying in front of the door to keep an eye on him, he removed the prosthesis with a groan and massaged his stump until the worst of the ache eased.

The ibuprofen had helped, but he considered taking something a little stronger. Then dismissed the idea. He didn't want to be less than alert while they were looking for Frank's killer.

Once he'd showered, he grabbed the crutches, made his way to the window and looked out. Even though it appeared the attacks hadn't been aimed at him, he couldn't help being on edge, antsy and worried about Jade.

"She's a cop," he told Sasha. "She's trained to take care of herself, right?"

Sasha yawned.

The fact that she had fellow officers watching her house was the only thing that allowed him to go to his bed and collapse on it in an exhausted heap.

Sasha settled herself on her bed next to him.

It was only when he was getting nice and comfortable that he realized he'd left his phone in the bathroom. With a groan, he sat up. Sasha jumped to attention. "Sasha, phone." He pointed to the bath. She ran to the room and disappeared inside. When she returned, she dropped his phone onto the bed next to him. He wiped the doggie drool off on his sleep pants and scratched her ears. "Good job, girl. Now go get in your bed."

Sasha obeyed. Sat there for less than three seconds, watching him before she got up and joined him back on the bed with a hopeful look. "Oh, fine," Bryce said. "You can stay, just don't tell Kristy."

He knew Kristy really wouldn't care, and he was glad for the company. When the dog realized he wasn't going to make her get down, she rolled to her side with a contented sigh while Bryce stared at the ceiling and let the grief flow over him.

He shifted and closed his eyes. Which brought Jade's beautiful face front and center in his mind. Someone had tried to kill her tonight and would have succeeded if he and Clay hadn't finished strapping the tree to the car and gone looking for her.

Jade. What was he going to do about her? She'd always gotten under his skin, even as a teen. He'd stayed away from her, thinking she was too young for him, but when he'd seen her that day at the college...

He sat up and slid his legs to the edge of the bed. Well, leg and a half. The half was a good reminder why he needed to stuff down any feelings he might have for

Jade. She deserved better. Someone whole. Someone who wouldn't be a burden to her.

Sasha raised her head and eyed him. "Sorry, girl. I'm restless tonight."

If he couldn't sleep, he might as well work. He sat down at the small desk in the corner and pulled the pad and pen over. He wrote everything he knew about what Frank was working on and names he'd heard the man say. When he finished, he sat back and read over it, disgusted to see it wasn't much. But he'd give it to Jade, and maybe she could make some sense out of it.

Bryce returned to his bed and lay down. Sasha raised her head once more, and Bryce thought she might very well be frowning at him.

He grabbed his phone and texted Jade. Are you awake?

No answer.

Okay, so I was thinking. Maybe we can decorate the tree sometime after lunch. Make an afternoon of it if you feel up to it. Just text me in the morning and let me know what you think.

He set the phone back on his end table and shut his eyes, praying he wouldn't dream, but knowing Sasha would wake him if he did.

# SEVEN

The next morning, Jade rolled out of bed with a groan. She'd slept late, but that wasn't the main reason for her audible protest at moving. Her throat ached, her head pounded, and she had sore muscles in places she didn't realize had muscles.

Popping more medicine for her aches and pains, she checked in with Captain Colson, but he told her nothing new had been learned last night about Frank. A call to the hospital informed her that Tony Swift had taken a turn for the worse and was in a medically induced coma.

For now, there was nothing to be done until he woke up—and she prayed he would—or one of the other detectives came up with a lead. "Take some time, Jade," her captain said. "Heal. You won't be any good to anyone if you're not a hundred percent. And that's not a suggestion. It's an order. I don't want to see you anywhere near the office today."

She grimaced, loath to admit he was right, but...he was. Fine. She'd take today and rest. Heal. Be with her family. She'd let the other detectives work the case and trust they'd keep her in the loop. And she'd check on Heather.

She read the text from Bryce once more and it made

her stomach hurt, but she couldn't put this off forever. He had to know about Mia. After an answering text to Bryce saying, After lunch sounds good, she walked into her kitchen to find a note on the counter from her father.

Sleep as late as you can. Mia is with us at the main house. Your watchdogs are being very vigilant so I'm comfortable that you're safe sleeping here.

God bless her parents. She honestly didn't know what she'd do without them. A glance out the window confirmed she still had her security on the house. It made her feel slightly better, but she was terribly confused as to why someone would attack her. Had it been just some random thing? Someone who'd been looking for an easy victim to rob? Or was the attack more deliberate?

Did they think because she was Frank's friend and a cop that he'd confided in her about whatever he was working on? That she knew something about dirty cops protecting that drug ring? She wished she knew something. Unfortunately, she didn't have a clue.

But if the attack was aimed at her, that meant the person had been following her and simply waiting for a chance to strike. She shivered at the idea and went to the den window to look out. Her small apartment overlooked the back of the property, with her parents' home to the left. She looked out in the distance to the sloping hill overlooking the large pond between her parents' home and the pasture beyond it. She'd always thought it would be a perfect spot to build a house. "Maybe one day," she whispered to herself.

Her phone chimed, bringing her back from her dreams of a life that didn't include someone trying to kill her. A text from Bryce. Tell me what time to be there.

A little after one. That would give her time to make herself presentable and make sure the medication had kicked in, have a chat with Jessica—and try to come up with a way to tell Bryce that Mia was his child.

See you then.

Jade dialed Heather's number, and her friend picked up on the first ring. "Hello?"

"It's me."

"Yeah, I kind of recognized the number."

A tiny smile curved Jade's lips, then fell away. "How are you this morning?"

"Awful. But my mom is here. So maybe slightly better than awful."

"Of course." Jade refused to be hurt that Heather hadn't wanted her to stay with her, but she could certainly understand the woman preferring her mother.

"Did you see the news this morning?" Heather asked.

"No. I just woke up about ten minutes ago. Why?"

"Another overdose. A teenager this time. She was found in the alley behind O'Sullivan's bar. Peter and Sarah snagged the case shortly after Frank was found." Her voice cracked on the last word, and she cleared her throat. "He was investigating the drug ring," she said. "They must have found out and killed him."

"Possibly," Jade said, "but what did he know? How did he even know who to look into? He had to have an inside source to even begin investigating, but who? And I know it wasn't you or me."

"Of course it wasn't. There's no telling," Heather said. "He had his secrets. But the police are releasing the house this afternoon and, as much as it'll kill me to be in there, I'm going to search it from top to bottom and see if I can find anything that will help us figure it out."

"You think there's something the crime scene unit will miss?"

"I won't know until I get in there and look."

"Of course. Do you want some company?"

A pause. "Maybe. I'll call you if I decide I need help or if I just want to do this alone."

Jade bit her lip, then sighed. "Heather, don't shut yourself off from people. From me. I just want to help. We all do."

"The problem is, no one *can* help." A sob slipped across the line and speared her heart. Heather cried, and all Jade could do was listen. Finally, her friend sniffed and fell silent. Jade waited, trying to think of what she could do or say and came up empty.

"Sorry," Heather said. "I'm sorry. Sometimes it just overwhelms me."

"No need to apologize. I know."

She heard Heather take a deep breath and let it out slowly. "All right," Heather said, "let's think about this. We've got access to resources Frank didn't. If he tracked down these drug runners, how come we haven't been able to yet?"

"I don't know, I just know the drug task force is working on it." Jade paused. "Bryce is coming over later. Do you want to join us?"

For a moment the line was silent. Then Heather sighed. "Maybe. How's that working out for you? Seeing Bryce again?"

"What do you mean?"

"I mean, he's Mia's father, isn't he? I'd think it'd be a little uncomfortable being around him again."

Jade froze, her insides turning to ice. She hadn't told

a soul who Mia's father was. "What makes you say think Bryce is Mia's father?" She forced the words past her lips, rather proud that she managed to keep her panic out of her tone.

"Something Frank said."

Her heart had done a fast thaw to thud out of control in her chest. "What exactly did Frank say?"

"Something about that weekend Bryce went to say goodbye to Kristy. Frank rode with him and said Bryce wound up spending more time with you because of your grandmother dying. He also said that he didn't remember Bryce returning to where the guys were crashing that night and that Bryce was tight-lipped when he showed up to go home. I did the math and it fits."

"You never said a word." If Heather had done the math, Frank probably had too.

"Wasn't my business." She paused. "So it's true?"

Jade closed her eyes and considered lying. But couldn't. "Yes, Heather. It's true."

"Are you going to tell him?"

"Of course I am."

"But you haven't yet." Another pause. "Why not?"

"When has there been an even halfway right time to tell him? When bullets were flying at the shooting range? Or maybe when someone was trying to strangle me in the Christmas tree lot?" And he had PTSD—which wasn't even the problem. The problem was his refusal to admit it. Silence from the other end of the line. Jade pinched the bridge of her nose. "I'm sorry. I didn't mean to snap, but I can't get into this right now, okay? As you well know, there's a lot going on and I just… I can't talk about this yet. Not because I don't want to tell you, but because I simply need to think things through before I say anything."

"Sure. Of course. You're absolutely right. I'm sorry I brought it up."

"It's fine," she said.

"Oh, by the way," Heather said, "I talked to Abby. She said as near as they can figure, the church was the last place Frank was seen."

"Any idea where he went after that?"

"CCTV footage shows him leaving the parking lot and turning east on Yancey Street."

"Which would take him toward home," Jade murmured.

"Or a lot of other places along the way. But, yes, since his car is in the garage, I'm assuming he got there safely."

Jade nodded even though Heather couldn't see her. "Then he disappeared from home."

"That's what it looks like, but Abby said she and a few uniformed officers are going to stop at businesses along the route between the church and his home to see if he stopped in. She said she's also going to ask for security footage from any cameras facing the street to see if his car passed by after his visit to the church."

"Sounds like she's got everything covered." Jade paused. "Unless someone came by and picked him up."

"Maybe, but there's no way to tell. His security system wasn't armed, and he doesn't have cameras."

"What about a neighbor's system? Maybe one of them caught something."

"Already thought about that," Heather said. "The officers who went house to house asked and no one has a camera facing Frank's home."

Well, that was just fabulous. Jade sighed. "Okay, thank you for the update. Hang in there, my friend. We'll figure it out."

"Yeah."

"And Heather?"

"What?"

"Please don't say anything to Bryce about Mia. I'm going to tell him, I'm just biding my time right now."

"You know I wouldn't say anything." Jade grimaced at the hurt in Heather's voice.

"I didn't mean to imply that you would, I just—ugh. You know people only say that to make themselves feel better. It's no reflection on—" She rubbed her eyes. "Never mind. I can't say anything right."

"It's okay, Jade. I know you didn't mean anything by it. I'm just super sensitive right now. We'll talk later, okay?"

"Sure."

Jade hung up, texted the information to Bryce, then went to get ready to face the day.

An hour later, she stepped into her parents' house to find the tree standing in the den ready to be decorated. The scent of fresh popcorn greeted her, and she drew in a deep breath. "Hello, anyone here?"

Mia's head popped out of the playroom at the end of the hall, and she bounded out to greet her. "Hi, Mommy."

Jade caught her up in a hug. "Hi, sweetie. Wow, you're getting heavy. Have you been eating popcorn?"

"No way. That's for the tree. I've been eating cookies."

"Oh, my bad. Of course."

"We *are* going to decorate the tree, right?"

"Yes, ma'am. As soon as one of Mommy's friends gets here." Just saying the words sent her anxiety skyrocketing. Bryce was coming here. He would meet Mia and she was going to have to explain everything.

"What friend?"

"His name is Bryce."

"Does he like kids?"

Jade blinked then let out a low laugh. "Yes." *As long as they don't belong to him.*

Her mom stepped out of the playroom with Gage right behind her. "Hello, darling."

"Hi, Mom."

"Gage and I are going to fix us some lunch. Mia, you want to help?"

"Sure."

"And you," her mother said to Jade, "need to go have a heart-to-heart with Jessica."

"I thought I might have to. Mia kind of gave me a heads-up last night."

Jade made her way down the hall and into the playroom, where she found Jessica sitting on a beanbag under the window. She was reading a book about teen sleuths who managed to get tangled up in a series of mysteries in their elementary school. "That was one of my favorite series when I was your age."

The girl didn't bother to lift her eyes, so Jade sat in the beanbag opposite her. "I know you're mad at me, and that's okay, but in this family, we talk things out."

Jessica finally looked up, jaw set, eyes shadowed. She didn't set the book aside. "You lied. There, we talked it out." Her gaze dropped back to the printed page, but Jade had a feeling she wasn't really reading.

"Well, technically you talked, but you didn't listen to my answer."

"What answer? That adults always lie about everything? It's okay. It's not my first rodeo, you know."

Jade raised a brow. "Where did you hear that expression?"

Jessica shrugged.

"Put the book down, please, and do me the courtesy of listening—just like I would do for you."

With a heavy sigh and a roll of her eyes, Jessica complied and crossed her arms to glare at Jade.

Instead of addressing the defiance and the attitude, Jade ignored it. "So, you're right," she said. "I didn't keep my promise about the Christmas tree and I owe you an apology."

The girl went still, and her mouth rounded in a silent O. Then she snapped her lips shut. "What?"

"I owe you an apology," Jade repeated. "Has no adult ever apologized to you?"

"Not that I can remember." The attitude had lessened quite a bit, and Jade slid her hand over Jessica's.

When the child didn't pull away, Jade took it as a good sign. "Well, that's lousy, honey. I think every adult in your life probably owes you an apology." She blew out slow breath, tossing words around in her mind, hoping when she strung them together, they'd make sense. "Look, Jessica, I have a very demanding job. One that I love. I'm good at it, too. And while I try to make plans—with every intention of following through on them—sometimes life derails those plans and I have to change them."

Jessica looked away. "Lolly said your friend was hurt."

"He wasn't just hurt, he died. It was Frank, honey."

The child flinched. "Frank? Frank died?"

Jade nodded.

The attitude was all gone and tears spilled over Jessica's lashes. "But why?" she gasped. "And how? Was it a car accident?"

"No, it wasn't a car accident. We're trying to figure out exactly what happened."

"I'm sorry," Jessica whispered. "Lolly didn't tell me that part."

"She was probably trying to protect you."

"I don't want to be protected. I just want people to be honest with me."

"I know." Jade held the child while she cried. When she pulled back and swiped her eyes, Jade pulled a tissue from the box on the small table under the window. "You have to remember, you're still a kid. And while you've probably been through more than most children your age, you're still a child. We adults want to protect you—well, the good ones in your life do. It's actually in the job description." She offered Jessica a small smile and brushed the child's dark curls away from her flushed cheeks. "And I don't mean that as a potential big sister, but as a *responsible* adult. Most of the adults in your life have really fallen down on the job, but Lolly and Pop and I, we're trying to change that." She tilted Jessica's chin until their eyes met. "And while I'll always want to protect you, I'll always be honest, too."

"No matter what?"

"No matter what." She paused. "But there might be some things I can't tell you. If I can't, I'll simply say that I can't tell you, but I won't lie."

The child turned into a missile, propelling herself into Jade's arms. "Thank you," she whispered. "I love you, Jade, and I'm sorry about Frank. I didn't know him for a long time, but he was always nice to me and Gage. I'll miss him."

Once again, Jade's throat went tight for the thousandth time in the last twenty-four hours. "I love you, too, sweetie, and thank you. He's going to be missed by a lot of people"

"I hope you get to be my big sister. I'd really like that."

Jade's heart flipped. "I would be honored to be your big sister."

A knock on the door startled her. Her dad stood there, and she thought he might be blinking back tears. "Hey, kiddo," he said to Jessica, "you ready to go for that horseback ride I promised you? Gage and Mia are all ready."

"Horseback ride?" Jade asked. "I thought we were decorating the Christmas tree?"

The child seemed torn. "Can we do both?"

"Absolutely. The day is ours to spend it how we decide."

"Then ride first and decorate the tree when we get back," Jessica said with a firm nod.

Jade watched her father and Jessica leave, and her smile faded. Well, one good thing about postponing the decorating. She could also delay telling Bryce about Mia. Or at least send her rehearsed speech through one more round of edits.

Bryce stood in front of Jade's front door with Sasha at his side. Two patrol cars sat in plain sight, but they hadn't stopped him from approaching the house. Jade must have given them a heads-up that he was coming and bringing a large dog.

So here he was, being a big old chicken about announcing his presence. He shifted and winced as pain arced into his thigh. His leg hurt from his overuse of it yesterday, but not bad enough to keep him down. He lifted his hand to knock, then lowered it. Why was he so nervous? What did he think was going to happen?

Well, the kids might not like him.

Ah…that was the issue. He was almost surprised to find himself that worried about it. But he was.

Sasha looked up at him as though asking him what the delay was. "Sorry, girl. I'm working up the nerve to ring the bell."

She leaned forward and pressed her nose against the lighted rectangle.

Bryce gaped. "Hey! Wait..." Too late. Chimes went off behind the door and he groaned.

*Bell.* He should have known better than to say that word while standing on the porch. When he'd been confined to a wheelchair, Sasha had been trained to ring doorbells for him. Apparently, she hadn't forgotten that part of her training. She sat and looked up at him, waiting for the praise. He scratched her ears with a sigh. "Good girl."

The door opened and Jade stood there dressed in jeans, a long red cable-knit sweater that reached midthigh and brown boots. She looked gorgeous, and it took a moment to find his tongue. "Um...hey. I'm not too early, am I?" Had she always been so striking?

"Not at all." She held out a hand to the dog. "Who's this?"

"Sasha."

Jade rubbed Sasha's nose, then worked her way to her ears. The animal groaned her appreciation. "Nice to meet you, Sasha," Jade said. Sasha lifted her paw, and Jade giggled. The sound went straight to his heart and took his breath away. "Wow. You're a very smart girl, aren't you?" She shook the paw. "The kids are going to adore you."

"Is it okay if she comes in?" Bryce asked.

Even though Sasha was a support animal, he never assumed she would be welcome in everyone's home—and Jade didn't know about Sasha's special role in his life.

"Of course." She motioned for them to enter.

He and Sasha walked past her and found themselves in a small living area. "It's cozy," he said.

When she didn't answer, he turned to find her standing to the side of the door, almost as though using it for protection, staring out into the distance. "What is it?" he asked.

She shut the door. "I thought I saw someone out near the barn."

Bryce's nerves stiffened. "What kind of someone?"

"I'm not sure." She snagged her weapon from the shoulder holster. "Stay here."

"Not likely."

Just like at the shooting range, she darted ahead, and Bryce ground his teeth. At least she didn't have to call for backup since it was sitting in front of her house. The thought made him feel only slightly better.

He followed behind her, leaving Sasha inside her den. He just hoped the dog didn't break anything trying to lie down in the small space.

Bryce navigated the steps and found Jade at the barn with the two officers who were watching the place. "We're going to walk through the barn," she told Bryce. "Can you hang back here and make sure no one comes out?"

"Of course." He pulled his weapon and held it ready.

One of the officers, Charlie, rounded the side of the barn, while Jade and Ricky entered the wooden double doors. Bryce waited, tension threading through his shoulders. He scanned the area, looking for anything that would tell him what Jade had seen. Nothing set off any internal alarms. He stepped closer to the door and glanced inside. She and Ricky walked sideways, back to back, sweeping their weapons up and across the barn. "Clear," Jade called.

"Clear out here!" Charlie called.

Bryce stepped into the barn, and Jade and her fellow officer joined him.

"You walked through the entire place and you didn't see anything?" Bryce asked.

She frowned and shook her head. "I guess I'm just paranoid."

"We're going to get set back up," Ricky said. He nodded to his partner and they left. Jade planted her hands on her hips while her eyes scanned the area.

Bryce did the same but didn't know what she could be looking for. "Everything okay?" he asked.

"I think so." She strolled down the center aisle, petting the horses' noses jutting from the stalls. At the office, she glanced inside. "Everything looks fine. I suppose I'm seeing things now." She turned and made her way back to the entrance, stopping at the steps that led to the horseshoe-shaped loft. "Ricky went up there and said it was clear." She shrugged. "So whoever or whatever I saw, it's not here now."

"You spent a lot of time in this barn growing up," he said.

"So did you."

He sighed. "Yeah. Lots of great memories. I miss those days." He narrowed his eyes. "That little secret room still there?"

"I guess." She smiled. "I haven't thought about that place in years. I'll have to show it to Mia one day. I'd do it now, but I'm afraid it would hold way too much appeal to her."

"Who?"

"Uh...one of the kids." She cleared her throat. "I sure do miss those days, don't you?" He'd just said he did. Her nervous tongue was going to get her in major trouble if she wasn't more careful. "I mean, I miss them, too. Especially summers when we just hung out, rode horses and went swimming in the pond. The four of us were inseparable."

"And we were all going to do big things with our lives. Remember that?"

"Yeah, I do."

He turned toward the entrance. "You know Frank had a big old crush on you at one point our sophomore year of college. I think you were sixteen or seventeen."

She gaped, all nervousness suddenly gone. "What? He did not."

"He did."

"Well, he sure never told me about it."

"He wouldn't."

"Why?"

Bryce shrugged. "He thought you were too young. He was going to give you a couple of years to grow up."

"I guess he changed his mind, because he never said a word."

"Guess so. When Frank told me he and Heather were engaged, I nearly fell over. He always said she needed someone to take care of her. I never guessed he'd be interested in that role. When did they get so chummy, anyway?"

She frowned, and they walked together back toward the main house. "Heather went to the police academy in Greenville but was determined to come back to Cedar Canyon and join the force. Only there weren't any jobs available, so she worked in a feed store until her current position opened up and they hired her. She and Frank started hanging out soon after she came home from the academy, and one thing led to another."

"I still can't see it, but what do I know?" He paused. "So, I know a little about your time in Charlotte. Can you tell me more?"

"What do you mean?" She pushed the garage door open and led him to the stairs that would take them back up to her place.

Did he dare ask? "Frank said you met some guy there. A guy he thought you were going to marry."

She looked away from him. "I thought I might, too."

"What's his name?"

"Lee Simpson."

"Why'd you break it off?"

She raised a brow and stepped inside her home. Sasha padded over to greet him while Jade tilted her head and studied him. "What is this? *Twenty Questions*? An interrogation? You're not with CID anymore."

Bryce grimaced. "I know. I didn't mean to sound like that." A pause. "Well?"

"Well what?"

"Why'd you break it off with him?"

Jade huffed a laugh and shook her head. "For a lot of reasons, Bryce. Too many to list, but suffice it to say, he wasn't right for me."

"Is he the reason you moved back here?" Bryce walked to her sofa and lowered himself onto it.

Jade took the chair near her fireplace. "Part of it. And partly to be near family. I…needed my parents' help…" A funny look flittered across her face before she shot him a tight smile.

"Help?"

"Look," she said, rubbing her hands together, then dropping them to her thighs. "I need to tell you something."

He wasn't sure he liked the sound of that. "What?"

"I...uh...whew..."

He frowned. "That's a real struggle. Just spit it out."

"I have a daughter."

# EIGHT

For a moment, Jade waited for him to respond, to react, to…something. Finally, he blinked. "A what?"

"A child. A daughter. Her name is Mia and she's five years old." Better to start simple. *I have a daughter* instead of *You have a daughter* or even *We have a daughter* was just…easier. If she had used *you* or *we*, she doubted his reaction would have been quite so…calm. "Bryce?"

"I…see." He sucked in a breath and raked a hand over his head. "Wow."

"That's it? Wow?" *Ask me*, she wanted to yell. *Ask me if she's yours.*

"Okay," he said, "well, I guess I understand why you moved back here. You needed your parents' help to take care of the baby."

"Yes, exactly."

"Frank never said a word."

"Frank apparently never said much of anything to you about me," she muttered.

"Sorry?"

"Nothing. Look, I told you that because—"

The door slammed open, followed by running footsteps clamoring up the steps and into the den. "Mommy? We're back! Can we decorate the Christmas tree now?"

Jade closed her eyes for a brief moment. When she opened them, Bryce looked pale. "Can we finish this later?" she asked.

"Of course."

Mia stopped when she saw Bryce in the den, and her eyes widened when she spotted Sasha lying in front of the fireplace. Then her attention swung back to Bryce and she grinned. "Hi."

"Hi."

"I'm Mia. Who are you?"

Jade's throat tightened. Mia had never met a stranger. Making a new friend—especially one who had a dog—was always at the top of her priority list.

Bryce rose and went to kneel in front of the little girl. "I'm Bryce, a friend of your mom's."

Mia's face fell. "Mommy's friend Frank died. Did you know him?"

"I did. He was my friend, too."

"I miss him. He took me and the twins to a birthday party, and he always brought me ice cream. It's very sad."

"Yes, it sure is." Bryce cleared his throat.

Mia stepped closer. "Who's that?" she whispered and pointed at the dog.

"That's Sasha," he whispered right back.

"Wow," Mia breathed softly. "Can I pet her?"

"Sure."

Bryce walked her over to the dog that looked like she could crush her with one paw. "She's ginormous," Mia said.

"Ginormous?" Bryce asked. "Where'd you learn that word?"

"Jessica."

"Well, this ginormous dog is a Great Pyrenees and

she loves kids." He directed her hand to Sasha's ears, and Mia scratched. Sasha's eyes closed and Mia giggled.

"She likes it," Mia said.

Jade watched the two, heart thundering, palms sweating, confusion swirling. Why would he think he'd be a lousy dad? He was amazing. Okay, so he'd only been interacting with Mia for all of three minutes, but still...

"So," Bryce said, "what's this I hear about decorating a Christmas tree?"

Mia's face brightened. "It's all ready. Lolly saved the popcorn from last night—well, most of it—and Gage and Jessica are trying really hard not to eat the rest of it."

Bryce raised a brow. "Just Gage and Jessica?"

"Well... I might be trying pretty hard, too." Another giggle escaped her.

"Then I guess we need to get down there."

"Are you going to help?"

"If that's okay with you."

"Of course. The more the merrier, my mommy always says."

He looked up and met her eyes. She tried not to blush, ordered herself not to, but the heat crept into her cheeks anyway.

"Does she, now?"

"Yes, but you have to bring Sasha."

"Well, then, how can I refuse?"

Apparently, he couldn't.

Together, the three of them walked over to her parents' side of the house and found her mother in the kitchen, popping more popcorn. "Hi, Mom, look who's here to help decorate the tree."

Her mother turned from the microwave, gasped, and threw her arms open as she hurried to him. "Bryce!"

He hugged her. "Hello, Mrs. Hollis."

"I'm so glad you're home." She leaned back and cupped his cheek as he looked down at her. "And I'm so sorry about Frank."

"We all are."

"More popcorn, Mom?" Jade asked.

"The other didn't last very long." She let Bryce go and returned to the microwave to pull out a yummy-smelling bag.

"I'm sure it didn't." Jade clasped her hands and looked at Mia. "Well, now, how about a little tree decorating?"

"I'll get Gage and Jessica," Mia said. "They're in the playroom." She darted down the hallway and soon returned with the twins. "This is Bryce," Mia told them. "He's Mommy's friend."

Gage studied him from under lowered lashes and Jessica frowned at him, but said, "Hi."

Jade forced some cheer in her voice. "All right, little people, let's have some fun." Mia cheered, Gage smiled and Jessica giggled.

Jade led the way into the den, and Mia picked up the remote and aimed it at the stereo system sitting on the bookshelf. Soon, Christmas music filled the house and ornaments hung from the tree. The children's faces beamed, and Bryce seemed to be enjoying himself.

Even Gage had gotten over his initial shyness and let Bryce lift him to place an ornament on a top branch.

Guilt slammed her that she was enjoying this time with her family while Heather was grieving. She should be there with her. She should be looking for Frank's killer. She should be *doing* something.

Bryce caught her eye and she gave him a tight smile. He raised a brow, and then his expression softened. "It's okay," he mouthed. Her heart settled a fraction. He was right. These kids needed her, and they deserved a happy Christmas.

When it was done, Jade stepped back to admire their work. "It's perfect, you guys."

"Hit the lights, Pop," Gage said.

The overhead lights went off and the multicolored bulbs covering the tree twinkled merrily.

Jessica walked over to hug her. "Thank you for this," the child said softly. "Even if this is all there is, it's already the best Christmas ever."

Jade's heart splintered, and she squeezed the little girl to her and kissed the top of her head. "I totally agree with that." Today had been a teaser, a sampling of what *could be*. And hit home it was exactly what she wanted. Her gaze went to Bryce, and the longing intensified. "All right, everyone. Dig in to the leftover popcorn."

Her phone rang as the kids raced to the bowl.

She stepped out into the sunroom for a little privacy. The snow fell on the other side of the floor-to-ceiling windows, and it occurred to her that she was too exposed. If someone were truly trying to kill her, she needed to take more care. She backed into the small alcove where the outdoor storage room was. It faced the house and shielded her from any possible prying eyes. "Hi, Captain."

"How are you feeling, Jade?"

"Okay." She just realized she still sounded pretty hoarse. "Not a hundred percent, what with the aches and pains, but I'm all right. What can I do for you?"

"Two things. First, I got a look at that security footage from the shooting. Unfortunately, it doesn't tell us much. The shooter was thin, and wore a flannel shirt and a green generic ball cap. Looks to be about five-seven or five-eight, but could be a couple of inches taller."

Or shorter. "So, that's a dead end."

"For now."

"And the second thing?"

"Looks like they're bringing Swift out of that coma in the morning. If you feel up to it, you want to question him?"

"Of course."

He paused. "I only met Frank a few times. This isn't a tiny town where everyone knows everyone, but it's small enough that I know the majority, and I liked Frank. What was he working on? Do you know?"

"The drug ring, sir. He was trying to figure out who the head person was." Well, that was true enough. She didn't see the need in telling him Frank suspected a dirty cop—at least not yet.

"Sounds like he got too close to figuring that out."

"Yes, sir."

"CSU couldn't find a personal laptop, and there wasn't much on his work computer. His boss said if there was anything on a computer, it would be his personal one. You know where it might be?"

She frowned. He was following this case awfully close. "I don't kn— Wait a minute. I saw it on that desk in Frank's den when Bryce and I went looking for him. I even tried to access it, but it was password-protected."

"I asked Heather and she said she didn't know where it was. Said Frank must have had it on him when he disappeared."

"No, that can't be right. I'll head over to his house and check."

"Do that and let me know what you learn from Swift."

"Will do."

She hung up and turned to find Bryce watching her through the glass doors. When she returned to the den, she quietly filled him in. "I need to get that laptop. I'm also thinking of going to see Heather."

"I'm not sure that's such a great idea. You've got security here."

She bit her lip. True. "All right, then I'm going to ask her to come over here and bring the laptop. She loves the kids. Maybe being around them will... I don't know... help. Somehow. I can take the laptop in tomorrow on our way to see Swift."

"It's worth a shot." He paused. "And I'd like to go with you in the morning to see Swift."

Jade frowned. "Why?"

"Because maybe the fact that I kept him alive until the paramedics got there will make a difference in what he tells us."

"Huh. Good point."

"Then I can tag along with you?"

"What are you going to do if I say no?"

"Come anyway."

"That's what I figured."

For the rest of the afternoon, Bryce alternated between watching his phone, checking the windows and playing with the kids—and watching Mia. He'd admit to doing the math in his head and wondering if she could be his. Every so often, he thought he saw a flash of... something...that reminded him of himself.

No, that was crazy. Jade would have told him.

Maybe he should just ask her.

But if Mia wasn't his, Jade would be horribly offended.

But if she *was* his...

Why hadn't Jade told him?

She would have, so obviously Mia wasn't his.

The turmoil continued to twist inside him, but he thought he hid it well.

Sasha didn't seem to be bothered by any kind of anxiety whatsoever. She lounged in front of the fire. Every so often, she'd wander to find the kids, checking to be sure all was well, then return to her spot and settle her nose between her paws.

The snow had stopped for now, but the last update from his weather app said it was supposed to start up again tomorrow.

Jade had slipped into the kitchen a few minutes earlier, and he could hear her on the phone once again. Not wanting to look like he was eavesdropping, but wanting to catch her alone for a few minutes, he slowly made his way into the kitchen.

"All right," she said. "Thank you for letting me know." She hung up and dropped her chin to her chest.

"What is it?"

She looked up. "I called Heather and asked her to pick up Frank's laptop and take it in to the captain."

"Okay, but that's not why you're so pale."

"The ME beeped in while I was on the phone with Heather. He just…um…finished with… Frank."

Bryce couldn't stop the involuntary flinch accompanied by a wave of grief. "And?" he asked.

"And basically, the autopsy confirmed what we already knew. The two gunshots killed him."

He swallowed and nodded. "What else?"

"There's no sign of a struggle. No bruises, nothing under his fingernails or on his hands. It's like he just stood there and let someone pull the trigger."

"Or he was taken by surprise?"

"Or that. But the bullets went into his chest. He was

facing his killer—which, to me, indicates he knew the person."

"Or at least trusted them." Bryce shook his head. "We really need to know where he went after he left the church. But we know he made it home because his car is there."

"Yes, but according to the detectives who've been working this, none of the neighbors remember *seeing* Frank come home. What if whoever killed him drove it there?"

"Then CSU will find something."

She rubbed hand across her lips and shook her head. "Today's been great and the kids needed it. If I'm honest, *I* needed it. My headache has finally eased, and I think my throat is feeling a bit better. Or maybe the ibuprofen is just doing its job, but…"

"But you're back at it tomorrow," he finished for her.

"Absolutely. If I didn't have full confidence in the detectives working the case, I would have been back at it today regardless of my head and throat. But truly, my brain simply won't stop. I've got to figure this out or go crazy."

He nodded. "Last night, I wrote some stuff down that Frank and I talked about. I keep going back to the day I told him I was coming home."

"What about it?"

"I sensed some hesitation on his part. Like he wasn't sure he wanted me to be here."

She frowned. "Why?"

"I think he was worried I'd come back bitter and angry and disrupt Kristy and the kids' lives or something. Or maybe yours and Heather's. Or his and Heather's. Who knows? Once he realized that wasn't the case—and he learned I was opening my own private investigation agency—he started acting normal again and wound up asking me if I'd help him with the story he was working on. He figured since no one knew anything about me coming back, I would be the perfect one to do this without arousing suspicion."

"How did he arrange for you to ride with Dylan?"

"He didn't. I did."

She frowned. "But why Dylan?"

"Frank had a list of names and gave them to me. He was looking at four cops in particular. I chose Dylan first because I knew him pretty well and figured once things went well with him, the other officers might not mind having me along so much—or suspect anything out of the ordinary. I just told them I was interested in being a cop and wanted to see how a small-town force worked." Which actually hadn't been a complete lie. He had been interested, just aware they'd never hire him because of his leg.

"And you're just now mentioning this?"

"I wouldn't have mentioned it at all if Frank wasn't dead," he said softly.

"Right."

"Who are the other three names on the list?"

He pulled the paper from his pocket and handed it to her. She glanced at it and the frown deepened. "You've got the captain on here," she said softly. "My boss."

"I was going to ask to shadow him next."

"I know all of them and can't see any of them being involved in cooperating with this drug ring."

"I've done a little background work on all four of them. To be honest, nothing really set off any alarm bells. I will say that the captain is in some pretty heavy debt from that new house he's building since he hasn't sold the old one yet."

She raised a brow. "He's building a new house?"

"Yes. A nice big one."

"Great. But a big house and debt don't automatically put him in the dirty cop role."

"I know."

"But it doesn't look good." She sighed. "Still, Captain Colson has a spotless reputation in the department. He worked his way up and is a decorated officer. There's no way I believe he's involved."

Bryce rubbed his eyes and shook his head. "I don't know. All I know is those are the names Frank gave me."

"Now I really don't know who to trust."

"I recommend you keep doing what you're doing. Talking to who you're talking to. If you change things now, it could make someone suspicious."

"Right."

"I'll keep digging into the background of the others, too."

"Mommy!" Mia's call from the kitchen had Jade pursing her lips.

"That child," she said. "She only has one volume setting. Loud."

He smiled. "She's a great kid. All three of them are."

"Thanks." She shook her head. "What is it, Little Bear?"

The sheer love in her eyes sent his stomach twisting into knots. She had a child. And the more he watched them together, Bryce would admit, he was envisioning what it might be like to be a part of that family unit. Having met Mia, the thought wasn't quite as terrifying as it might have been once upon a time. He cleared his throat and stepped back when Mia burst into the room.

"Lolly and Pop are going out for dinner with friends

while they can get through the snow. Can we have pizza for dinner and watch a movie? And can Bryce stay?"

Jade hesitated.

"I'm game if you are," Bryce said. The words tumbled from his lips before he had time to filter them. What was he doing? She was a mother. He never planned to be a father. The last thing he should be doing is spending time with them. But…he wanted to.

"Ah…sure," Jade said. "That's fine, hon."

Happy squeals filled the room. She darted to Bryce and wrapped her arms around his leg for a hug. "Thank you, Bryce!" Before he could react, she was gone, darting back to the kitchen. "She said yes!"

Bryce shook off the amazing feeling that had come with Mia's spontaneous affection and wanted to smack himself. He should have left while he had the chance. Now he was committed to spending the evening with Jade and three kids.

Why he found himself smiling, he had no idea.

When thoughts of Frank and the fact that someone might be after Jade for something she knew—but didn't know she knew—resurfaced, the smile faded, and he placed a hand over his weapon. He didn't want to use it—but he would if it meant keeping Jade and her family safe.

# NINE

Jade stared at the television while her mind whirled. She and Bryce sat on either end of the sofa. Mia had tucked herself up against his side while the twins settled for the beanbags on the floor. Bryce seemed quite content to let the little girl snuggle against him, and she caught him casting glances at Mia every so often.

She loved the movie they'd chosen, but she couldn't seem to focus. Mia's complete adoration of Bryce threw her. Even the twins had warmed up toward him. When she put the kids to bed, she was going to have to tell him about Mia.

A knock on the door was a welcome distraction. "That's the pizza!"

The others barely looked away from the screen. Including Bryce. Chuckling, she walked to the door and looked out. And blinked. She threw open the door. "Heather? You came! Get in here out of the cold."

Once Heather was inside, Jade gathered the woman into a hug. Heather returned it, then stepped back. "I see you've got protection out there. What's going on?"

"Just a precaution."

While Heather hung her coat on the rack in the corner, Jade explained about the incident at the tree farm.

Her friend gaped. "That's crazy!"

"Tell me about it. Did you take the laptop over to the captain?"

"No, I couldn't find it. Which is weird."

"What's even more weird is that it was there the day we went looking for him."

"You went to his house?"

"Bryce and I did. Bryce even suggested Frank's password would be Heather."

She huffed a short laugh. "He'd never do something so obvious."

"Yeah, you're right. We didn't figure out the password, but the laptop was there when we left."

Heather rubbed her head. "I don't know where it could be, then." Jade frowned but led her friend into the den. Heather stopped abruptly when she saw the other four.

"Oh no, you didn't tell me this was like a family night thing. I'm interrupting." She backed up. "I'm sorry. I'll just come back later."

"Absolutely not. We're going to break out the board games when the movie is over and eat pizza. Join us, please."

Heather hesitated. Mia got up and ran over to wrap her arms around the woman's legs. "Stay with us, Aunt Heather. It'll be fun."

More hesitation, then Heather sighed and bent to kiss the child's head. "Well, how can I refuse that?"

"Exactly," Jade said. "Besides, you *are* family."

Two hours later, the kids were tucked into bed, and Heather sat in the recliner, petting Sasha, her eyes distant. Bryce nodded that he was going into the kitchen to give them some privacy.

Jade sat across from her friend. "How are you doing?"

Anger flared in Heather's eyes before she looked

away. "Not good, Jade. I don't know what to do with myself now. The captain won't let me work the case, of course. I'm rattling around between two houses, looking for anything that would give us a clue as to who killed Frank, and I—" She spread her hands. "I don't know what to do."

"Take up painting again," Jade said softly.

"What?"

"Maybe it's a stupid suggestion, but I haven't seen you paint in ages. Maybe it will help. I'm not trying to say it'll distract you, but it's always been an outlet for you."

Heather sighed and raked a hand over hair that needed to be washed. "I've been so busy with work and…the wedding…" She drew in a shuddering breath. "What is it with me and men? My first fiancé left me practically at the altar and now Frank—" Tears spilled over her lashes and onto her cheeks. "It's not fair," she whispered. "None of this was supposed to happen. How could he do this to me?"

"I know. But you're strong. You survived that jerk and went on to prove it was his loss for leaving you. This isn't Frank's fault. He didn't *want* to leave you."

"But he did, didn't he?" The flash of fury faded as quickly as it appeared. Heather sighed and shook her head, swiping the tears from her pale cheeks. "Sorry. It doesn't matter whether he did or didn't. He was working a story that got him killed."

"And now he needs us to get him justice. Keep fighting, Heather." She walked over to kneel in front of her friend. "Keep fighting and together, you…we'll…heal from this loss, too."

Heather jumped up and Jade fell back onto her hip. The woman reached down and helped her up. "Sorry. Thank you. I don't know why I came here. I guess I just needed to vent a little. And... I'm angry at him," she whispered. "For letting this happen."

"I know." Jade hugged her once more. Then Heather slipped out the door, climbed into her car and left.

"Everything okay?" Bryce asked from the door of the kitchen. Sasha stood at his side, her big head swinging back and forth between him and Jade.

"No, not really. She's hurting."

"We all are."

"No, I mean, she's *really* angry. She was engaged once to a guy named Chance Little. He waited all the way up until the rehearsal dinner to back out of the wedding. Heather was devastated."

He winced. "I didn't know."

"But she managed to overcome it with the help of her friends and family. And Frank," she said slowly. "Frank was a great friend to her. Maybe that's when their friendship developed into something more. I don't know. But this...losing him? I'm afraid it might be too much for her. I think she's not just angry at the person who killed him but at Frank for taking on something so dangerous and leaving her out of the loop." She shrugged. "After the funeral, she's going to need us more than ever. Whether she realizes it or not."

He nodded, and started to say something when Jade's parents walked in. After a round of thanks for watching the children, he and Jade and Sasha stepped outside. It was cold, but clear. The snow had stopped, but the ground was covered in white. Bryce started to his car then turned back. "Jade, I..."

"What?"

"Is..."

She lifted a brow when he stopped.

"Does Mia live with your parents or you?"

She sighed. "My parents, mostly. She has a room in our apartment, of course, but with my work hours—and the twins' arrival—she's been staying with Mom and Dad more than with me. I don't necessarily like that, but it's the way it has to be right now—although maybe not as much as it has been—but she likes staying with Jessica and Gage, and I don't fight her on it. Mom and Dad are going through the process to adopt them, so Mia is beyond excited. She's already started calling them her brother and sister even though that's not technically correct. It doesn't matter. We all want them in the family." She ducked her head and let her eyes roam the landscape. "I love this place. It's my home—and Mia's. But I'm a single parent and a cop. I've had to accept that the combination comes with certain limitations—and that includes having my parents take care of Mia a lot."

"They don't mind."

"No, they don't."

"But you do?"

She scrubbed a hand over her face. "Sometimes. I wonder if it's the best setup for her. If it's stable enough. If running back and forth between two places is any way for a little girl to grow up."

"I know I've only seen Mia for a few hours, but she's an amazing kid. She's confident and outgoing and very well adjusted. I'd say whatever you're doing, you should keep doing it."

Jade huffed a short laugh. "Thank you. That means a lot."

"Today was wonderful," he said. "Thanks for allowing me to be included."

"You're welcome. I'm glad you wanted to be."

His eyes dropped to her lips, and her heart nearly stopped. His head started to lower. Her chin lifted. Sasha stepped between them and gave a low woof. Bryce let out a laugh, cleared his throat and stepped back. Heat flamed in her cheeks, and she ducked her head. He tilted it once more and let his lips cover hers. Jade froze for a brief moment and then allowed herself to enjoy the moment, taking comfort in his presence and the gentle exploration of his kiss.

Reality intruded. She owed him the truth. He must have sensed her emotional withdrawal, because he pulled back. "Everything okay?"

"Yes, I just…maybe we shouldn't… I mean, you don't want—" kids? He'd kissed her, not asked her to marry him.

"Right. I understand."

Did he? Well, that was good because she wasn't sure she did. And now she'd made the moment awkward in her usual clumsy, fumbling way. "Bryce, I'm—"

"It's okay, Jade. I'll see you later," he said.

"Of course. Be careful going home."

"You too."

"Right. I'll try not to trip as I walk the fifty or so steps to my apartment above the garage."

He rolled his eyes and the awkwardness faded.

"Sasha, tell Jade good-night." Sasha dropped to the ground, crossed her paws over her snout and closed her eyes.

Jade let out a delighted laugh. "That's precious."

"Good girl, Sasha."

The dog bounded to her feet, tongue lolling, obviously very pleased with herself. Jade scratched the animal's silky ears one more time before Bryce loaded her into his truck.

Jade breathed a sigh and it wasn't until his car was out of sight that her pulse started to settle.

Then she noticed the cold. The darkness that pressed in just past the lights of the barn. She shivered in spite of the new officer who'd replaced the other shift. Because whether she wanted to admit it or not, she could feel someone out there watching her. Waiting.

Waiting for the moment she was vulnerable and alone, like in the tree lot. *I don't know anything!* She wanted to shout the words into the stillness. *He didn't tell me anything!*

Would it do any good? Would the person believe her? She doubted it.

Bryce couldn't sleep. He'd almost asked Jade about Mia's father, but had chickened out at the last minute. As much as he tried to convince himself that Jade wouldn't keep such a major thing from him, he simply had to know. "So, ask her tomorrow," he muttered and punched his pillow. Sasha raised her head and eyed him from her bed across the room. She'd chosen her bed over his after he'd awakened her more than usual. Funny, how she knew when he was just restless and when he needed her to pull him out of a nightmare.

He shut his eyes, but his mind continued to spin.

Mia was five. But on what end of five? A young five? Or an about-to-turn-six five? And had she been born when expected or had she been a preemie? Knowing her due date and her actual birthday would tell him a whole lot. He was a PI. How hard would it be to find out that kind of information? Easy peasy. But he didn't want to do it that way. It would feel too much like sneaking around behind Jade's back.

"Because that's kind of what it would be," he muttered.

Sasha sighed and lumbered out of the room.

Jade had said she'd met someone while in Charlotte and had even dated the guy long enough to make people wonder if she would marry him. Which meant it was highly likely that Mia wasn't Bryce's child.

But the timing of it all just wouldn't leave him alone.

"Ugh!" He'd rolled out of bed and pulled on his clothes before his eyes landed on the clock. Almost midnight. He lived barely five minutes away from Jade's place. He could be there almost as fast as he could blink. Sasha returned to the room, leash in her mouth. She dropped it on the floor and stared at him.

He couldn't help the short laugh that slipped from him. "You want to go for a run, huh? Or you think I'm the one that needs to?"

Sasha yawned and blinked. He gave her an ear scrub, and she licked his hand. "You're the best, you know that?" Bryce texted Jade. Are you awake?

While he waited for her to answer, he let Sasha out, then back in.

After fifteen minutes of no answer, he had to assume Jade was sleeping. Which is what he should be doing. He hung the leash back up. "Sorry, girl, my leg's not feeling so great. We'll go first thing in the morning, okay?"

He checked his phone again. Still no answer from Jade.

With impatient hands, he undressed and crawled back into bed, promising himself he would bring up the subject of Mia's parentage first thing on the way to the hospital to question Swift.

Maybe.

Sasha settled back onto her bed with a disgusted huff. "Sorry, girl."

She ignored him. He couldn't say he blamed her. Five more minutes of tossing and turning and he gave up. He dressed, grabbed the leash, and found Sasha in the hall. "Neither one of us is going to get any sleep until I know Jade is okay, so let's just go check, make sure she's okay and then maybe we can both get some sleep. That sounds all right to you?"

Sasha bounded to the door.

Jade blinked out of sleep. Disoriented, confused—and grumpy. The high-pitched beeping reverberated in her brain and she rolled over, trying to block the sounds of the alarm clock, not ready to get up yet.

A loud boom shook her home and sleep fled. She shot straight up. Mia! She shoved the covers away and stood. Smoke billowed through her open door and she got a face full. Her lungs burning and spots dancing before her eyes, she dropped to the floor to find the smoke hadn't fallen that far yet. Jade drew in a breath and, on her hands and knees, scrambled down the hall to Mia's room and found it empty, the bed still made. Terror shot through her for a brief second before she remembered Mia had wanted to stay with Jessica. The kids were at her parents'. But were they safe? Smoke swirled but wasn't as bad here as it was in the hallway and Jade's room.

Jade darted into Mia's bathroom and grabbed a towel. She soaked it with water, then wrapped it around her nose and mouth. A quick look under the cabinet revealed the small fire extinguisher her dad had put there when she'd first moved in.

She snatched it and then headed back into the smoke-filled hall, looking for flames. Nothing yet. She made her way into her small den area. Again, a lot of smoke, but no fire. At the front door, she unlocked the dead bolt and twisted the knob.

Nothing.

With a shaky hand, she pulled harder. Then yanked. The door refused to budge.

*What?* She laid her palm flat against it.

Hot—and growing hotter by the second. Her stomach twisted. Sudden flames shot through the bottom and into the room, sending her stumbling backward. With a harsh yell, she pulled the pin on the extinguisher and fired it at the base of the door.

*Please, please, please, God, help me.*

Another loud boom shook the structure, and she went to her knees, dropping the towel and the extinguisher. In the kitchen, the wall facing the wooded area out behind her home crackled with bright orange-and-blue fire. Fear choked her along with the smoke. She snatched the towel back to her face, but it would only work for so long.

She had to get out—or call for help. And warn her parents. Her phone.

Jade spun, ran back to her bedroom and grabbed her cell phone from the end table. Squinting against the haze, she made her way to the window, threw it open and dialed her parents' number.

"'Lo?"

"My apartment's on fire. Get Mom and the kids out."

"What about you?"

"Going to get the ladder and go out the window. My door's too hot."

She hung up and dialed 911. Her room was above the detached garage that jutted out below her. The roof of the garage sloped slightly down, but even walking to the end of that, it was a long drop. "Oh Lord, help me."

"911. What's your emergency?"

"Darlene? This is Jade. My house is on fire!"

"Sending units now. Can you get out?"

"Working on it."

"Stay with me."

Jade darted to the closet, eyes and throat burning, and reached for the emergency fire escape rope ladder. Her hands fell on empty space. What? Confused, but with no time to figure out where the ladder had disappeared to, she sprinted back to the window and looked down. The jump probably wouldn't kill her, but it would hurt.

Her bedroom was on the opposite side of her parents' house, so she couldn't see the state of their home. Where had the fire started? How far had it spread? She looked back over her shoulder. With her bedroom near the kitchen, the flames had already eaten their way into the hallway, blocking her door, the smoke growing thicker, barreling toward her.

"Jade! Jade! Are you in there?"

"Dad!" He rounded the corner of the house and looked up, his gaze frantic. Bryce appeared behind him. "The ladder's gone and my door is jammed," she cried. "I can't get out!"

"Can you wait for me to get the ladder out of the barn?"

"Yes. Hurry!" Jade swung a leg over the sill and scrambled onto the roof, smoke pouring out after her. She coughed and paused to drag in a lungful of the fresh, cold air.

"I've got it," Bryce said. He took off. In less than a minute, he was back, leaning the tall ladder against the gutter.

"What about your side?" she asked. "Mom and the kids?"

"Already got them out and down near the barn. Fire trucks are on the way."

"Where's the cop who's supposed to be guarding this place?" Bryce called.

Good question.

Bryce held the ladder still, and she stepped out onto the first rung. "Careful!"

Sirens reached her, and she could see flashing red-and-blue lights in the distance. They'd be here within a couple more minutes. The flames licked into her bedroom, and all she could think was that she was so grateful Mia hadn't been there.

Eyes, lungs, throat burning, she scrambled down the ladder and into Bryce's waiting arms. He hugged her, then pushed her away while her dad grabbed the ladder. She checked her parents' place and saw that the flames had worked their way to the middle of their shared covered walkway, but hadn't yet reached their house.

"Hurry," she whispered to the truck not yet there. "Please."

Her phone squawked, and she lifted it to her ear. Dispatch. She'd forgotten about her. "It's okay, Darlene, I'm out."

"Trucks should be there in less than a minute."

Bryce led her over to the barn, where she found Mia, Jessica, Gage and her mother waiting and watching the flames. Her mother grabbed her in a hug. "I was so scared."

"I know, Mom, but I'm okay." Mia reached for Jade, and she swung the child into her arms. Where's Travis?" she asked. "The officer watching the house?"

Her mother shook her head. "I don't know." Tears tracked her dusty cheeks, and she gathered the children closer to her. They all appeared shell-shocked, and Jade's anger burned hotter than the fire in front of her.

The fire trucks arrived and had hoses going wide open within less than a minute. *Please save my parents' home, Lord, please.*

# TEN

Standing next to a shivering Jade, Bryce kept an arm around her while Dylan Fitzgerald wrote notes in his little black notebook as fast as Jade could talk. Someone settled a blanket around her shoulders, and he helped wrap it around her before tucking her up against his side again. In spite of the circumstances, he couldn't help but note that she felt right being there. He could keep her next to him for the rest of his life and he didn't think that would change. The thought sent chills that had nothing to do with the weather down his spine. *Keep your distance, Kingsley. She deserves better than you.*

Like someone with two good legs and a whole lot less emotional baggage. Someone who wanted kids and could be the kind of father they deserved. Mia reached for him. Surprised, he took the little girl from Jade and settled her against him. The feel of her slight weight in his arms had his throat closing. When she laid her head in the crook between his neck and shoulder, his heart filled with a tenderness he'd never be able to put into words. He had to look away from her while he processed the fact that someone had put her in danger tonight. Her and Jade and the entire family.

His gaze landed on Sasha, who stared at him from the

front seat of his SUV, where he'd left her during all the chaos. Her displeasure at being separated from him was clear in her brown eyes. He sighed and made a mental note to slip her an extra treat a little later.

"Jade!"

The shout snapped Bryce's gaze around to the man climbing out of his vehicle.

Jade stopped midsentence and turned. "Captain?"

If Bryce thought he was wound tight before, that was nothing compared to the new layer of tension the man's arrival added. Frank had listed his name as a possible dirty cop, and Bryce decided his friend had been right to do so.

Captain Colson sure was keeping tabs on things. And, of course, he would to a certain extent, but to Bryce, he was *overly* interested. Was he worried about what Jade might uncover in her search for Frank's killer? If that was the case, then it was very possible the man was responsible for all of the attempts on Jade's life. Was he also responsible for protecting drug dealers who were making and selling their poison? For putting this precious family in danger? He hoped he kept his thoughts hidden from his face, but he didn't plan to let the man out of his sight for as long as he was in close proximity to Jade. His hold tightened around Mia, and she snuggled closer with a little sigh.

"Captain Colson," Jade said. "I'm surprised to see you here."

He raised a brow. "Surprised? I still get out of the office occasionally. I heard the call go out over the radio. I'm glad to see you're okay."

"Thanks to my dad and Bryce."

Bryce shifted Mia to the crook of his left arm and shook the captain's outstretched hand.

"Looks like someone has it in for you, Hollis," the captain said.

"No kidding."

"You know why?"

She went still, then sighed. "I have a couple of theories. I don't know if they're even close to being right, though."

"Care to share?"

"I can do that, but I'd prefer not to do it here."

"All right. My office sometime tomorrow if you feel up to it?"

"Yes, sir."

He nodded. "You and your family have someplace to stay? I don't think it's safe to remain here. Not with someone so determined to get to you."

She coughed and took a swig of water from the bottle Bryce had slipped into her hand. "I agree. My aunt lives in Boone. I think they'll head to her place. My dad's already been on the phone, getting the horses taken care of. Thankfully, my parents' home wasn't damaged, so I plan to stay here."

"Hopefully, it won't take them long to finish the investigation, and we'll know how this fire started." The captain's phone buzzed, and he glanced at the screen. "Nathan McDonald is on his way."

"The fire marshal?"

"I gave him a heads-up on my way over here. With everything going on, there's no way I believe this was an accident."

"No," she said. "It wasn't. My front door was jammed somehow." She paused. "And there were two mini-explosions."

Bryce blinked. "Explosions?"

"One in the kitchen and one outside my front door."

"I can understand the one outside your door, but how would anyone get inside to plant a bomb without being seen?" the captain asked.

"Good question," Jade said. "Unfortunately, I don't have a clue. My ladder was missing, too."

"Ladder?"

"It's a rope ladder I kept in my closet in case I had to get out from the second floor. Like tonight. I don't think Mia knew it was there, but it's possible she could have moved it. She, or one of the twins, but I highly doubt it. Whoever broke into my place must have done it while I was out either last night or today sometime, because I feel sure I would have noticed them. I didn't see any sign of forced entry when I got home tonight. And my door wasn't jammed. That came after I went inside for the night. Absolutely nothing triggered any kind of alarm that someone had been in my place." She shrugged. "I just don't know."

"Did anyone find Officer Kane?" Bryce asked.

"Out cold, sir. Found him beside his patrol car with a goose egg on the side of his head and a two-by-four beside him. Paramedics are transporting him to the hospital now. Overheard them say something about a possible fractured skull, but thought he would most likely be okay in time."

"Unbelievable," the man muttered. "All right, thanks. Let's get Mr. and Mrs. Hollis and the kids escorted to wherever they're going tonight."

Bryce turned Mia over to Mr. Hollis, then kept an eye on everyone in the vicinity of Jade. "I think you should go with your family," he told her.

"Not a chance."

"Jade—"

"I'm not leaving, Bryce. Please don't try to get me

to change my mind." She shook her head. "I'm more determined than ever to catch the person responsible." She pointed toward her smoldering home. "What if Mia had been in there? Or what if all three of the kids had? Because sometimes we have slumber parties on my den floor."

"Jade, you can't play the what-if game. You'll just run in circles." She swiped a stray tear, and his heart thundered with the need to comfort, to reassure her. "This is just a blip in the road. A speed bump. Once this person is caught, everything can return to normal."

But the child who'd slept so innocently in his arms had Bryce convinced that would be a new normal. The burning question about whether or not Mia was his wouldn't leave him alone.

"I can't stand the thought of them in danger. The kids, my family. Any of them."

Bryce pulled her into a loose embrace and let out a low breath when she didn't pull away. He rested his cheek on her sooty head. "This can't go on much longer. Whoever is doing this is getting bolder. Sooner or later, he—or she—will make a mistake."

She nodded, then stepped out of his embrace and straightened her shoulders. "You're right about one thing for sure. This can't go on much longer. It has to end. I'm getting back on top of this investigation, and I'm going to figure out what someone thinks I know—and why that scares them badly enough to want me dead."

Thirty minutes later, Jade pressed fingers to her tired, burning eyes. Her parents' home hadn't been touched by the blaze, which was a real blessing. Her place, however, was a disaster. Unable to get in for so much as a change of clothing, she dropped her hands from her eyes and riffled her mother's closet. Thankfully, her mom dressed young for her age and loved jeans and sweatshirts. The jeans would be slightly too big, but a belt would take care of that.

Showered and dressed in fresh clothes, Jade made her way into the den, where she planned to tell Bryce he was Mia's father. It had to be said. She found him asleep on the couch. A very restless sleep. He tossed one way, muttered something, then turned and lashed out with his hand. Sasha jumped up from her spot in front of the fireplace, but Jade, recognizing the signs, hurried over to him while staying out of reach. "Bryce," she called softly. "Wake up."

His muttering ceased, but the frown said he was still dreaming. Sasha moved closer and nudged his thigh.

Jade touched his shoulder and leaped back in case he decided to swing at her. He thrashed, muttered something and kicked out. Sasha hurried to him and nudged her snout into his face.

"Bryce, wake up now." Jade's firm tone—in addition to Sasha's actions—must have penetrated his mind somewhere in the depths of the nightmare, because his eyes opened, and he sat up blinking.

His eyes focused on her for a moment before recognition dawned. "Oh, hey, sorry. I didn't mean to doze off." His gaze dropped to the dog, who now sat next to him, hovering over him.

"It's okay," she said. "You were dreaming."

"Yeah." He scratched the dog's ears, and Sasha started to visibly relax.

"A nightmare," Jade pressed. "Do you have them often?"

"It was just a dream, Jade."

"It was more than a dream."

"No, it wasn't," he snapped.

Her heart went cold. "Right."

Bryce scrubbed a hand over his head. "Sorry, it was just a stupid dream. It's not important. The big question is, are you all right?"

"I think so." Physically, anyway. Emotionally, she'd just taken another hit. He obviously had some PTSD issues and refused to admit it. It also looked like Sasha was much more than a well-trained pet. She was a service dog.

Jade took a seat in her dad's recliner and leaned back. If she thought she could sleep, she'd lift the footrest and close her eyes. Instead, she frowned. "I forgot to ask you what you were doing here so late. I thought you'd gone home."

"I did, but I couldn't sleep. My mind wouldn't shut off and I…" He shrugged and looked away from her. "Sasha was getting disgusted with me for all of my restlessness and was insistent that I do something to alleviate it."

"Sasha, huh?"

"Actually, yeah. She gets her point across really well without saying a word. Anyway, I thought we could talk. When I pulled up, I heard your dad yelling for you."

"I'm glad you came back." She dropped her head and pressed her hands to her cheeks. "I can't get the sound of those explosions out of my head."

"I know the feeling. I still hear the sound of the IED that went off and caused me to lose my leg."

"Is that what you were dreaming about?"

He stiffened, then stood. "I'm going to get some water."

"I'll get it." He wasn't going to budge on telling her about his dream. "Someone planted those bombs in my house," she said, "and they had to have some kind of timing device."

"Because they went off at a specific time. What about a remote detonator?"

"Maybe. ATF will take a look and be able to tell us more." She paused. "It had to be someone I know, Bryce." She walked into the kitchen and looked in the refrigerator. The open concept allowed her to talk to him at the same time.

"Why's that?"

"Because the person had access to my home." She took two water bottles back into the den and handed him one. He'd seated himself once more on the couch. "Someone who wouldn't be considered a stranger around here—although with as many people as we have coming and going, that's going to be hard to narrow down. There's trainers and boarders and riders and feed people, the vet…" She waved a hand. "The list goes on."

"So it wouldn't be hard for someone to get on the property disguised as help or whatever."

"No, not hard."

Brows furrowed, he nodded and swigged the water. "But to get inside your home, that's another matter altogether. Do you hide a key anywhere?"

"No. In fact, I hate to admit this, but I rarely lock the door."

"Why wouldn't you lock it?"

"Because Mia goes back and forth so much that I just don't." She walked to the door that led to the covered walkway and gazed at the burned remains of her home. Sickness twisted inside her. "This is the only way to get to my place from here without going outside. There's a ground floor door from the garage that leads inside to stairs. If you go up those stairs, you'll find yourself at my front door."

"But you keep that locked, right?"

She shrugged. "Most of the time."

"Seriously? With what you do for a job and you don't lock your doors? How is that even possible?"

She turned. "Look around, Bryce. We're in the middle of twenty acres. If someone were to come up the drive, we'd know. And like I said, when someone comes up, it's usually someone we know."

"What about when you're not home? It wouldn't be too hard to figure out your family's schedule and check when you're working. And what about someone sneaking through the woods? You know as well as I do where those woods come out."

She bit her lip. "The main road that goes into town."

"Exactly. Someone could park a car…"

"Yeah, I've thought about it, too, but we've lived out here since this place belonged to my great grandparents. Not once has there been an issue."

"Times are different now."

"Boy, are they." She shook her head, her mind only halfway on the discussion. The other half was trying to decide what to do now about telling Bryce that he was Mia's father. PTSD and a man in denial. Great. Been there, done that—and she had no intention of revisiting that place.

"Captain Colson was on that list Frank gave me." Bryce said. "He thought the captain was much too involved in the drug ring investigation." He paused. "What's your impression? Do you really think he could be guilty?"

She groaned. "I don't know. Of course I don't want

to think so, but..." A sigh. "I don't know what to think about him—or any of the others on that list."

He studied her. "You need a break."

"I had a break. I'm still having that break thanks to the person who tried to strangle me and burn down my house. Captain's orders." She stuck her bottom lip out. "I feel like I've been benched for something I have no control over." Jade rubbed her eyes. "Can we talk about something else? I think I need some distance before I can come back and try to sort everything out."

"Sure. Tell me about Mia's father, then," Bryce said softly.

Jade jerked. "Why?"

"I'm curious. He must be a great guy for you to fall in love with him."

She blinked. "He has his good points."

"Does Mia see him?"

"No." Jade drew in a steadying breath. She didn't want to lie, but she couldn't tell him the truth now, not yet. Not until she figured out exactly where he was in dealing with his PTSD issues. "She doesn't." She paused. "I was thinking we should go to Frank's tomorrow after we talk to Tony Swift."

Bryce studied her, and she wondered if he'd insist on talking about Mia's father. After several seconds, he finally gave a short nod. "All right."

"I know Heather's there and going over everything, but it's possible she's too close to this. Maybe we'll see something she can't."

"I think that sounds reasonable."

"We'll call her on the way to the hospital in the morning."

"She looked bad, Jade. I'm worried about her."

"I know. I am, too. I'm glad her mother is with her. Maybe Heather'll talk to us a little more tomorrow."

He rubbed a hand down his face. "She hasn't said when the funeral is. You think she's even thought about it?"

"I think she has. I also think she may be avoiding it." Jade swallowed and looked away. "I'll call Lisa tomorrow, too. She and Frank were really close. I'll ask her what the plan is."

"Good idea. In the meantime, why don't we get some sleep?"

"You're staying here?"

"There are four officers surrounding this house and a fire crew just outside making sure nothing sparks another blaze." He stood and walked over to kneel in front of her—albeit a bit awkwardly with his leg—and take her hand. "Frankly, I wouldn't care if the entire police force was out there with the national guard. I'm not trusting your safety to anyone else anymore. I'm going to keep you safe, Jade."

She gaped, then snapped her mouth closed. "But—"

He pressed a finger to her lips. "But nothing. Don't get me wrong. I know you're capable and fully able to take care of yourself. I have no doubts about that. And this isn't some caveman thing where I think you need me to protect you. It's something I *want* to do. I *want* to be here." He paused. "Because while you may not need my protection, I need to give it. I wasn't there for Frank, but I really want to be here for you."

Jade swallowed, her heart pounding from the sudden surge of adrenaline. That look in his eyes spoke volumes. Then it was gone, and he was pushing off the arms of the recliner to his feet. She let her gaze stay locked on his, wanting to believe him—and scared to let herself fall for another guy in denial about his PTSD.

"Thank you," she said.

"Get some sleep, Jade. You're going to need it."

"I will. You too."

"Of course."

She paused. "I feel horrible that my family is going through this. I can only pray this doesn't hurt my parents' chances of adopting the twins."

"Well, right now, they're safe, and that's all that matters. If we can get this cleared up ASAP, then I would think their plans to adopt would be fine."

"Right. So, let's figure this out ASAP."

"See you in the morning, Jade."

"'Night, Bryce."

She went into her parents' bedroom and crawled into their bed. Tears hovered on her lashes and finally spilled over onto the pillow. *Please, dear God, let us get to the bottom of this and please, keep my family safe. And give me wisdom about whether or not to tell Bryce about Mia. I know I need to, I just...can't. Yet. Tell me when, Lord.*

# ELEVEN

The night had passed without any more trouble, and Bryce had listened as Jade talked to her parents, then each child, before hanging up and calling the hospital to check on Tony Swift. "Still in a coma?" Jade had said. "I thought he was waking up." Pause. "All right, thanks. Call me if something changes." She'd hung up and turned to Bryce. "He took a turn for the worse during the night."

"I gathered. So... Frank's?"

"Yeah. Frank's. I still want to know what happened to that laptop."

Now they were on the way with a police escort. Apparently, the captain wasn't taking any more chances on someone getting to Jade. Which made Bryce wonder if Captain Colson was really a concerned boss? Or a man who wanted it to look like he was going all out for one of his own?

While Jade drove, Sasha stretched out in the back of the SUV with her nose on her paws, eyes shut. Bryce called Frank's sister, Lisa, who answered on the second ring.

"It's Bryce, Lisa. How are you holding up?"

"Well, to be honest, not all that great, but I've got Chad. He's being my rock."

Her husband, Chad, and Bryce had graduated high school together. "I'm glad," he said.

"Frank was just here, you know. He spent last weekend with us, playing with the kids and just…being Frank."

"I know. He told me."

"And now he's gone. I want the person who killed him caught and put in prison." A sob rippled through the line, and Bryce closed his eyes.

"I'm sorry, Lisa, I wish I could do more."

She sniffed and blew her nose. "Just make sure the police are staying on top of this."

"They are, I promise. Especially Jade."

"I know," she whispered.

"Hey, could I ask you a quick question?"

"Of course."

"Have you talked to Heather?"

"No, I haven't." A sigh. "I've been so wrapped up in… everything, we haven't connected other than through voice mails. I need to call her again."

"Okay, well, if you think of anything, anyone Frank might have talked to recently, will you call me or the police?"

"Of course. You don't even have to ask that."

"I know, but it helps me think I'm being proactive."

A squeal in the background reached his ears. "George, don't hit your sister! I've got to go," Lisa said. "I promise to call if I think of anything."

"Thanks, Lisa."

When Jade pulled to a stop in front of their friend's house, Bryce couldn't stop the shudder that ripped through him. It hit him hard that Frank was gone forever and wouldn't enter his home again.

Heather's car was parked out front. Their police escort stopped behind them.

Jade led the way to the door, and it opened before they had a chance to ring the bell or knock. Heather stood there in a baggy long-sleeved T-shirt and paint-stained jeans. "Hi."

"Hi," he said. She looked awful. "Have you slept at all?" he asked.

She sniffed and let out a whispery laugh that held no humor. "Not really."

Jade pulled Heather into a hug and simply held her for a moment before letting go. The three of them, followed by Sasha, walked into the house, and Heather gestured them to the couch while she took the wing-backed chair next to the fireplace. Sasha settled in front of Bryce's feet.

"It's hard to sleep," Heather said. "Or eat. Or breathe."

A tear tracked down Jade's cheek and she swiped it away. "Where's your mother?"

"I sent her home."

"What? Why?"

One of Heather's shoulders lifted then fell. "Because I just can't stand being around her pity. And the looks she gives me." She shivered. "I can't even really describe it. A cross between how-could-you-let-this-happen and you're-so-pitiful-because-you-lost-another-one. It was really getting to me."

"It's not pity, Heather, it's compassion," Jade said. "People just want to *help* you."

"Help me? Help me?" Her voice rose with each word. "There is no help for me! Frank's gone and there's nothing I can do about it! Nothing anyone can do about it!" She dropped her face into her palms, and Bryce rose to his feet and went to kneel in front of her.

"Heather," he said softly, "you're right. Frank's gone. And you're right, there's nothing any of us can do to make it hurt less—except maybe find his killer. Maybe. It might not take away the pain, but at least we can sleep knowing we did that. We can do that for him—and us. Get him the justice he deserves."

She waved a hand. "I don't even care. What difference does it make if we find who did it? It's not going to bring him back." A sob slipped from her. "I just want him to come back."

Bryce pulled her to him while Jade stood and paced the length of the den. After several minutes had passed, Heather's sobs ceased, and she drew back to palm her sunken eyes. "Sorry. I didn't mean to do that."

"It's okay," Bryce said, "I think you needed to."

"Why are you guys here? What do you think you can find that I haven't?"

"Who knows?" Jade said. "We have to try."

Heather waved a hand. "Have at it. His office is down the hall on the left. Feel free to start there. I've looked through a bunch of stuff and found nothing but some random notes about this story he was investigating."

"Notes?"

"Yes, but they don't make much sense to me."

Bryce raised a brow. "Show us."

In Frank's office, Heather stepped to his desk. "This is exactly how he left it the day he disappeared. There's nothing on it that means anything to me."

Jade pulled on a pair of gloves, walked over to the desk, and began going through it. Bryce watched her work, impressed with her professional demeanor. It had to be hard to portray it, but she did so with a tight jaw. Finally, she stepped back, notes in hand. "I don't think these will tell us much, but we'll take them with us to study." Hands on her hips, she looked around, eyes landing on the end table next to his bed. "That looks like a file cabinet."

Heather frowned. "Maybe. I didn't look there, but I think Finn and Trent did." Finn Bennett and Trent Young. Two other detectives they worked with on a regular basis.

Jade pulled open the drawer. "Files—which one would expect to find in a file cabinet." She thumbed through them while Bryce and Heather watched. Then she removed them one by one and set them on the bed. "Aha," she breathed.

"What?" Bryce moved closer, and Heather leaned in.

Jade pulled a file from the back of the drawer and stood. "This." She walked into the kitchen and set it on the table, then opened it. "Pictures."

"Of what?" Heather asked.

"People. Cops. Places with cops." She passed each picture to them. Bryce studied the first one with Heather looking over his shoulder. "I know this place," he said. "It's an old warehouse not too far from the mill where Frank was found. Looks like some kind of drug buy going down."

"Yeah...and look who's in the background behind those two."

Heather nodded. "Dylan Fitzgerald."

Jade narrowed her eyes. "Dylan? He wouldn't."

"Apparently he would," Heather said. "Looks like he found out that Frank was on to him."

"And he had to shut him up," Jade whispered. She shook her head. "We need to bring him in ASAP, but...if he's involved, who else might be?" She pulled her phone from her pocket and hesitated, trying to figure out the best move to make next.

"I can't believe this," Heather said. "This was worth

risking his life for? Risking our future for? Why wouldn't he tell me?" Her eyes narrowed. "Do you think he suspected me, too? Unbelievable." She sniffed and swiped a stray tear.

"No," Jade said, "I don't think so. There aren't any pictures of you in these. He just probably didn't want to make you feel like you had to be suspicious of everyone you worked with."

She shook her head. "Who knows what was going through his mind? Look, you two, I hate to cut this short, but I've got to go."

Jade blinked, her thumb hovering over the last button that would put her through to her captain. "Where are you going?"

Heather sighed. "I'm meeting with the funeral director."

"I thought Lisa was taking care of that," Bryce said.

"She is, but we finally talked and I told her I wanted to be there. 'Til death do us part, right?" She grabbed her purse from the end of the sofa. "I'll talk to you later. I want to know what you get out of Dylan. Lock the door when you leave, please?"

"Sure," Jade said.

Heather left, and Jade let out a low breath. She cleared the phone screen and looked at Bryce. "What if the captain's involved?"

"Then telling him about Dylan isn't going to help much."

"What about my captain's boss? Commander Chris Nelson?"

"You trust him?"

She huffed a short laugh. "Before all of this, I would have trusted my captain and Dylan, but yes, I trust him. I think I'm going to have to. Not every cop in the department is dirty. We just have to make sure we find the ones that are."

"Trial and error? Sounds dangerous."

"Gut instinct, too. The commander is a good man." She paused. "But then, so is the captain. Argh!"

"I think telling the commander is a good place to start."

She nodded. "All right, then let's do that." Jade headed for the door, and Bryce fell in behind her. She opened the door and twisted the small knob to ensure the door was locked when Bryce pulled it shut behind him. The sun broke through the clouds, warming her face in spite of the chill of the day. She enjoyed the moment while Sasha bounded ahead toward the car.

A loud crack sounded. Wood splintered from the door frame, and Jade ducked. "Get down!" She hadn't finished her yell when Bryce grabbed her hand and pulled her across the front lawn toward the SUV.

"Sasha, car!" At Bryce's order, the dog bounced after them, making a beeline for the SUV.

Another pop, and a bullet plowed into the ground to Jade's side. Bryce pushed behind the vehicle, lost his balance and toppled next to her. She grabbed his wrist and yanked. Between her pull and using his good leg for more momentum, he was finally with her, safe behind the cover of the vehicle.

The police officers scrambled to return fire. One drove in the direction of the shooter, his tires squealing on the concrete. Calls went out over the radio. Another bullet slammed into the side of her SUV. "I can't believe this," Jade gasped. "Where are the bullets coming from?"

"Hard to tell."

A crack and the back window of the patrol car parked behind her ruptured. "There," she said. "I'm going after the shooter. I'm really tired of getting shot at and people trying to blow me up or burn me alive."

Hunkered against the wind and hopefully any more incoming bullets, Jade started to her feet.

Only to find herself on the ground again, pulled down by Bryce who hovered over her. "Stay down! Stay down!"

Jade froze for a split second at his harsh cries. "Bryce!"

*"Incoming!"* He lifted his hand as though he held a radio and not a cell phone.

"Sasha, in," Jade said. The dog obeyed. "Down, girl." She lay on the seat, taking up most of it. "Bryce, get in the car and keep your head down." He moved, and she breathed a sigh of relief. Sasha nosed Bryce. Then licked his face. He shuddered, eyes still glazed, but aware. "Bryce, can I hug you?" Jade asked, knowing that sometimes a hug worked to help calm someone in the midst of a PTSD moment.

He glanced at her and nodded. She scooted closer and wrapped her arms around him, squeezing him as tight as she could. When she felt him relax, she slowly released her hold and lifted her eyes to his. He blinked and for a split second, horror registered. Then embarrassment and finally, shame. "It's okay," she said. "You had a PTSD moment. A flashback."

"No. No, I didn't." But he leaned his head into Sasha's massive shoulder and shuddered.

The denial shattered her heart, the pain so intense, she gasped. "Right."

The officer who'd gone after the shooter drove back into the driveway. Jade climbed out of the SUV, leaving Sasha to comfort Bryce. A very-much-in-denial Bryce.

After the all clear was given, Jade walked over to hear what the officer had to say about his chase. She wondered how she would ever be able to tell Bryce that Mia was his. Because once she did, he'd want to see her on a regular basis. He might not want children, but there was no doubt in her mind that he'd step up and "do the right thing." And there was no way she'd ever feel comfortable leaving him alone with the child. *Her* child.

She shoved aside the thoughts. "What happened? How did the person get close enough to shoot the window?"

Officer Johnson turned. "It was most likely a long range rifle."

"Had to be," Bryce said from behind her. She glanced at him. He still looked a little pale, but his set jaw said questions wouldn't be welcome.

"The shots came from the tree line," Johnson said.

Jade rubbed her eyes. "I'll start working on my statement."

Bryce caught her eye, started to say something, then shook his head. "Yeah, I will too."

Jade headed to her vehicle, a sick feeling twisting in her belly. Once they found Frank's killer and whoever was trying kill her, she'd say a final goodbye to Bryce and pray her broken heart could heal yet again.

# TWELVE

Bryce paced the lobby of the police station while Sasha sat against the wall and watched him, head swiveling, nose twitching, ears raised. She was on high alert in the new environment, so in tune to him that he couldn't help dropping onto the bench next to her to place a hand on her head. "It's all right, girl, you did great. Thank you."

She licked his hand and seemed to relax a fraction. He'd had a flashback. His first one in over a year. Worse, he'd lied to Jade about it. Not intentionally. The denial had just been the first thing to pop out of his mouth. Probably because he was in absolute shock that he'd had one and didn't want to admit it to himself, much less someone else. Especially not Jade. He dropped his head into his hands and forced himself to think it. *I had a flashback. I had a flashback.*

And Jade had witnessed it, and this time he couldn't disregard the incident as a bad dream.

The fact churned his stomach. He'd thought he was past all that, but everything that had happened in the last few days must have brought it all back to the surface.

Jade was still in the commander's office, filling him in. Bryce pulled his phone from his pocket and dialed the man who'd helped keep him on the right side of sanity.

"What do you want?" Titus growled in that gravelly voice Bryce had missed.

Bryce smiled, most of his tension and anxiety draining away for the moment.

"Nothing you've got, old man." Titus Renfrow. Former Army Ranger turned amputee, turned alcoholic, turned AA mentor, turned counselor. A man who understood exactly what Bryce was going through. He could picture him leaning back on two legs of the old leather straight back chair, daring gravity to do its worst.

"Bryce, my friend," the voice softened to a low rasp, "really good to hear from you, son."

"Thanks, good to hear your voice as well."

"What's going on?"

"I had a flashback."

A pause. "Well, at least you admit it."

"After I lied about it."

"I see. So, what are you going to do?"

Bryce pinched the bridge of his nose. "Tell her I lied."

"Her?"

"Yes. Her."

"I see. And?"

"And put it behind me so I can move forward, looking to the future and not living in the past."

"Well, glad to see our sessions weren't a complete waste." Another pause. "What triggered it?"

"Someone shot at me."

"What?" Bryce thought he might have heard the chair thump to the floor. "Why did someone shoot at you?" Bryce gave him the condensed version, and Titus let out a low whistle. "You sure do like to live in the adrenaline zone, don't you?"

"Seems like it always finds me."

"Where was Sasha?"

"She was there, doing what she does." Which was probably why the flashback didn't last as long as some of the others had. Okay, that was a positive.

"How long was it?" Titus asked.

"Ten seconds? Maybe a little more. Could have been slightly less."

"Then I'd say that's not too bad, considering you were shot at."

So they were thinking along the same lines. "Yeah."

"You going to be okay?"

After a deep breath and some serious thought about the question, Bryce released the air in a low sigh. "Yeah. I think I am."

"You've already done the hard part."

"Admit there's a problem."

"Right."

Jade opened the door to the commander's office and stepped out. "Thanks, Titus," Bryce said. "It helped just knowing you'd pick up the phone."

"Anytime."

"I've got to go. Talk to you later."

"Give Sasha my love."

Bryce smiled. Sasha had been to every session and had won the crusty man's heart. He hung up and waited for Jade to approach. "I think we've got everything in the system," she said. "I've turned over Frank's notes and the pictures to the commander, and he's going to be looking into Captain Colson and the others. In fact, he's already sent someone to pick them up and have them escorted to an interrogation room."

"Are you going to be doing the questioning?"

"No, the commander wants to do it."

"So, now what?"

"We're back to hurry-up-and-wait mode, but it's not a mode I'm comfortable with."

He lifted a brow.

"I want to hear what they have to say for themselves."

"So…?"

"I'm going to request us to be allowed to watch the interrogation."

With permission received, she and Bryce settled themselves behind the two-way mirror.

The commander sat across from Dylan, hands clasped in front of him. The pictures Bryce and she had found in Frank's file cabinet lay facedown in front of him. An open file folder lay next to the pictures.

Dylan twitched nervously in his seat, popping his knuckles and rubbing his nose. "What's this about, sir?"

"Captain Colson is tied up for the moment, so I told him I'd take care of this. Officer Fitzgerald, from what I can see, you have an exemplary record."

"Yes, sir."

"But, since there's no report of you doing any undercover work, I need to ask you about these." The commander flipped one of the pictures over and slid it across the table in front of Dylan. One by one, he did the same with the others. Jade knew each picture showed Dylan in some way interacting with known drug dealers.

"Can you explain them?"

Dylan leaned forward and frowned. Even from his vantage point, Bryce could see all of the color leech out of the man's face. For a moment, he sat frozen, then sighed and dropped his head into his hands. When he looked up, the commander was waiting. "Looks bad, doesn't it?" Dylan asked.

"What would you think if you were sitting in my chair?"

"Probably exactly what you're thinking, sir."

"We've also run your financials."

"I want a lawyer."

"And that's your right. I'll let you make a phone call." The commander stood.

"Wait." The commander paused while Dylan fidgeted a second longer. Finally, he raked a hand through his hair. "If I help you bring down the ring, will you put in a good word for me with the DA?"

Commander Nelson settled back into his seat. "It depends on how helpful your information is and if it really does lead to the dissolution of the ring and the capture of the top people involved. You have no idea how bad I want to bring this ring down." His hand curled into a fist on the table. "My best friend's son is in the ICU thanks to an overdose of the stuff that's being brought into this city."

"Well, that explains why he and Captain Colson are following this case so closely," Jade said.

"Will Dylan face charges of murder?"

"I don't know. I imagine that will be brought up as a possibility. Although if he helps as much as he says he can, then I would think he might get a much lighter sentence."

At the commander's insistence, Dylan called his lawyer while the commander spoke to the district attorney. When Nelson returned, he said, "The DA's willing to work with you and your lawyer if this leads to the arrest of those involved in the drug ring."

"All right," Dylan said with a short nod, "let's do this." For the next hour, he spilled everything he knew about the people involved. Thankfully, he cleared Captain Colson in the process. "One last thing," Dylan said. "There's a big shipment coming in tomorrow night around ten o'clock. An eighteen-wheeler full of drugs at the old warehouse behind the bank."

"You're sure?"

"Of course. I'm the one who set up the location since it's part of my beat tomorrow night. I'm supposed to make sure it's clear for the deal to go down."

Commander Nelson closed his notepad. "Why do this, Dylan? You have a spotless record. You have a beautiful family and, on the surface, this just doesn't make sense."

Dylan closed his eyes. "My wife, Julie, has a gambling problem," he said softly. His lids lifted, and the sheen of tears in his eyes flipped Jade's heart sideways. "She got into debt with one of the guys in the drug ring. Drugs, gambling, and gun running are what these people do best. When this guy learned she was married to a cop, he came to me and told me Julie's debt would be paid if I'd look the other way—and he'd let her and my kids live."

"I'm guessing things escalated from there to setting up the meetings?"

"Yeah. Yes, sir." He swallowed hard and ran a hand over his face. "I know you're wondering why I didn't ask for help."

"It crossed my mind."

"When I was approached, they already had someone on my kids' school and someone outside Julie's work, and they'd put ten grand in my bank account.

"If I'd told a soul…" He shook his head. "Doesn't matter now. I have to say I'm relieved—and terrified. Please, Commander, don't let them hurt my kids."

The commander narrowed his eyes. "They won't get to your family. As long as you and your family do what we ask. You have my word on that."

"He is something of a victim, isn't he?" Bryce murmured.

"Yeah. I can't say I wouldn't have done the same thing in his shoes."

The commander stood and paced the room for a good five minutes before he took his seat and leaned forward to look Dylan in the eye. "Okay, here's the plan. We're going to put surveillance on your wife and kids, make sure they're safe while not tipping off any of those involved in the ring. You're going to be on duty tomorrow night to make sure this goes off without a hitch. Once the deal's done, we'll move in."

"Sir, I want to help, I do. But these people are more than just dangerous. They're killers. They have no respect for life. If they think I've turned, my family—and possibly anyone around them—is dead. Regardless of protection." He used his sleeve to swipe the sweat from his forehead. Jade noticed the fine tremor in his hands.

"This isn't my first time doing this, Fitzgerald. I know what I'm doing and I work with a good team. You're absolutely positive none of my other officers are involved in this?"

"I'm positive—or at least, I think I am. I can only tell you that I've never seen anyone else on the force at the meetings."

"All right then." The commander swept the pictures and the file folder into his left hand and leaned in. "Now that we've got that settled, you said these guys were killers."

"Yes, sir."

"Then who killed Frank Shipman, and who's trying to kill Jade Hollis?"

"Frank?" Dylan spread his hands. "I don't know. If I did, I'd tell you, but that one was a surprise."

"He was working on a story related to this drug ring.

He's the one who took those pictures of you. I'd say that gives you motive."

Dylan flinched. "Maybe so, but I didn't know those pictures existed until you just showed them to me." He shook his head. "I've given you everything on this drug ring, but there's no way I'm going down for Shipman's murder. I didn't do it, and I don't know who did."

"Then who wants Jade Hollis dead so bad?"

"Again, I don't know." He paused. "Unless it's the person who was in the mill when she found Frank's jersey. Maybe they think she saw them."

"It's a thought," Bryce murmured to her.

"It is, but I think it's a long shot," Jade said. "I was attacked from behind. I never saw a thing."

"Still, you never know."

"True."

The commander stood and shut off the recording device. "Someone will be here soon with a transcript of this conversation for you to sign. You can discuss this with your lawyer, and I'll go fill the DA in on everything. I don't want anyone to know about this meeting. You're going to walk out of here like everything is just fine, you understand?"

Dylan nodded, his eyes on the table. "Thank you, Commander."

"We'll be monitoring everything you do. You wait two hours before you leave this building."

"Yes, sir." Another swallow that sent his Adam's apple bobbing. "Thank you, sir. I'm sorry…about everything."

"I'm risking a lot here, Dylan. I'm trusting that you want to make things right. This will go a long way towards doing that."

"I know. I won't let you down."

Commander Harrison stared at his officer for a few

more seconds before he gave a low grunt and stood. Then he walked out without another word.

"He's stepping out on a limb here," Jade said. "If Dylan runs…"

"He won't. He did what he did out of love for his family. He won't stop now."

When the door opened to the observation area, Bryce turned. Captain Colson nodded at Jade. "Looks like we're going to be planning a sting for tomorrow night."

"Looks like," she said. And while she was ready to bring down the drug ring, she couldn't help feeling frustrated that they didn't appear to be any closer to finding out who killed Frank—and who wanted her dead.

Jade picked up the picture of her and Mia from the mantel and couldn't hold back the surge of love that swept over her.

*God, please, end this.*

Jade replaced the picture and stomped into the kitchen just as her cell phone chimed. She snagged it from her pocket. "Captain?"

"Glad you answered. I've got some news on your little fire."

"You mean the one that's destroyed my home?"

"Yeah." He ignored her sarcasm. "Looks like you were right. Arson investigators found evidence of explosive materials."

Even though his statement wasn't unexpected, chills still danced up her arms. "What kind?"

"The kind that turns household items into bombs."

"I see."

"They also found traces of rope fiber outside your door and on the railing. You said you couldn't get out."

"The door opens inward. When I pulled, nothing happened."

"That's because someone tied it shut," he said. "Wrapped a loop with a knot around the knob, then around the stair railing, effectively trapping you inside. At least, that's the deduction. There wasn't a whole lot of rope left."

"It fits," she said. While Jade knew someone had rigged her door, hearing it stated as fact turned her stomach.

"The lab is working with the explosives, trying to get any prints off the remains, but don't hold your breath."

A knock on the front door startled her and sent her heart racing. "Someone's at the door, Captain. I'd better get it."

"You know who it is?"

Jade peered out the window. "Yes. Bryce and his dog."

"Okay. He's got clearance."

"Yes, sir. Thank you."

"Watch your back, Hollis. You're one of my best detectives, and I don't want to lose you."

The words settled in her heart, and gratitude filled her. "Appreciate that, sir."

"Answer the door. I'll be in touch if I learn anything more."

Jade hung up and opened the door to find Bryce with his hands in his front pockets, head slightly lowered, and looking up at her through his upper lashes. "Hi."

"Hi."

He cleared his throat. "Could I come in?"

She stepped back and led them into the den, where Sasha claimed her spot in front of the fireplace. Bryce chose the sofa. "I owe you an apology," he said.

"An apology?"

"I wasn't completely honest about everything."

Jade stilled. "Okay."

"I actually do have PTSD. And, as you've probably already figured out, Sasha's a service dog." He drew in a deep breath and let it out slowly. "The truth is, I've been in counseling for several years, learning to cope. One of the things I've discovered is that it doesn't help to deny its existence—as much as I might like to."

Jade blinked, slightly stunned at the admission and almost at a loss for words. "I'm sorry," she finally managed. "I know that's a hard thing, but I'm glad you're getting help."

"Losing part of my leg devastated me. It meant losing all of my hopes and dreams and facing a whole new reality. A new way of living, walking. Everything. I was very angry and bitter for a long time."

"I think that's understandable."

He shot her a small smile. "I've finally allowed myself to agree to that, but old habits and feelings sometimes rear their heads. And..."

"And?"

"And having you witness one of my moments was humiliating." He looked away, and Jade's heart pounded. Never in a million years would she have thought they would have this kind of conversation. Guilt hit her hard. She'd judged him based on someone else's issues. She'd automatically assumed he would be the same as Lee Simpson. He didn't deserve that. What he did deserve was the truth. "Thank you for trusting me enough to tell me."

"Yeah."

"Because I haven't been completely honest with you, either." She drew in a fortifying breath. "Bryce, I need to tell you something. About Mia."

\* \* \*

He froze for a brief second, and then his gaze met hers. "What?"

"She's…"

"She's what, Jade?" His pulse ratcheted up a few notches.

"Yours, Bryce," Jade whispered. "She's yours."

The breath left him in a rush, and all he could do was sit frozen. When he finally found his voice, he said, "That's why you wanted me to get in touch with you six years ago?"

She nodded.

"Frank didn't give me the message," he said. "I promise."

"I know that now."

"When did you find out?"

She shrugged and rubbed a hand over her forehead. "Not too long after you left. For several months, I walked around in denial, but I really did intend to tell you after I got over the shock of it. When I asked Frank why you weren't calling, he always had a legitimate-sounding excuse—like you were on a mission, and then it was that you were recovering from being injured. And then, after Kristy said she finally heard from you, but I didn't, I thought you were ignoring me and… I was hurt. So eventually, I just quit trying."

Feelings he couldn't identify warred within him. "Why did you wait so long to tell me now? We've been together nonstop for the past few days. Why haven't you said anything?"

"Why do you think?" she cried. "You really have to ask that?"

Shame engulfed him, overpowering the initial anger at her delay in telling him. "No, I guess I don't."

"In addition to your denial about your PTSD, you don't want kids, remember? You like kids as long as they belong to someone else, *remember*?"

Her agitation cut through to him and he nodded. "I remember." He paused. "You've done a beautiful job with her," he finally said softly. He had no right to be angry that she'd waited until now to tell him.

She swallowed and shook her head. "I had a lot of help. I couldn't have done it without my parents."

He sighed. "I'm sorry I wasn't here."

"I am, too, but it's not your fault. You didn't know, so no taking on undeserved blame, understand?"

"Yes, ma'am. I'll do my best." He shook his head. "I'm still very confused about Frank keeping this from me, though. I can't think of any good reason he'd not pass on your messages."

"I don't know, either."

"I think I'll ask Lisa."

"Good idea. I don't want to be mad at a dead man, but I'll admit, I am."

"Yeah." He drew in a breath. "I want to see her, Jade. I want to tell Mia I'm her father." She bit her lip and he frowned. "What?"

"If I…we…tell her," Jade said, "she's going to want to see you—on a regular basis. Probably more than that in the beginning as she'll be totally obsessed with the whole idea. You don't want to be a father, remember?"

"You keep saying that, but it's…" He swallowed and looked away. "It's not that I don't want to be a father. It's just that I'm not sure I'd be a very good one."

Jade stood and paced from one end of the room to the other. "Well, then that's something that you need to decide, because once we tell her, there's no going back."

"I know. I know." He stood, too. "When you confirmed my suspicions that she was mine, my first reaction was joy. My second was absolute terror," he said. "I might as well admit it since I'm coming clean on everything."

"Take some time and think about it," Jade said. "A lot of time if necessary. It's not a decision to be made lightly and not one that has to be made immediately."

Bryce walked across the room and took her into his arms, noting how right she felt there. He kissed the top of her head and stepped back. "Thank you for not hating me."

"I could never hate you, Bryce." Her gaze clung to his, and he knew that she was worried. He also knew he'd take the time to think about what being Mia's father would entail before jumping feetfirst into the deep end. Because Jade was right. Once they told Mia, there'd be no going back. He'd be a father—in every way that counted. Which meant he'd be seeing Jade a lot. The thought didn't bother him. Not at all.

# THIRTEEN

Bryce stood in front of the mantel, looking at the picture of Jade and Mia. Mia. His daughter. His *daughter*. A person, with thoughts and feelings and her whole life ahead of her. She was a part of him, and already he wanted to know everything about her. There was no way he could just walk away. From either of them.

He raked a hand over his head, his decision made. Not that it had been much of a decision. The moment Jade had said Mia was his, he was already making plans to spend time with her. And Jade. Assuming tonight went like it was supposed to.

Just letting you know that all is well right now, Jade texted. In position and waiting.

While he appreciated the update, Bryce wasn't happy that Jade planned to participate in the sting. Not because he thought she wasn't capable, but because she'd been injured, and one day off wasn't enough recovery time. If her job didn't require her putting her life on the line, that would be one thing, but it did, and she needed to be alert and on top of things.

However, he'd been unable to talk her out of going, so he'd keep himself busy while waiting to hear if she would finally be safe and Frank's killer was in custody.

He dialed Lisa's number.

"Hello?"

"It's Bryce, Lisa. How are you doing?"

"I'm...not good."

"I know. I shouldn't have asked."

"No, it's not just about Frank's death. I found his journal. He left it here last weekend when he stayed with us."

"He left his journal behind?"

"Trust me, I was incredibly surprised. He would only have forgotten to grab it if he was distracted. Which he was."

"You're not the first person to say that. Tony Swift, the owner of the shooting range, said Frank had been in a lot lately and seemed to have something on his mind."

"Exactly. I left him a message that I had it, but he never called me back. I'd put it in the drawer of the nightstand in the room he uses. With all of the craziness of the last few days, I'd forgotten about it. George went in there a little while ago and found it." She cleared her throat. "I...ah...opened it up and read a few pages." She paused. "Bryce, you spoke to Frank a lot since coming home. Did he ever say anything about calling off the wedding?"

Bryce stilled. "No. Why?"

"It's one of his last entries. He said he was marrying Heather for the wrong reasons and was going to talk to her about calling it off. I think that might be what had him so preoccupied over the last few weeks."

"It could be, but he didn't say a word to me."

"He wouldn't unless he'd talked to Heather first."

"Of course not." Now *he* needed to talk to Heather. "I don't think Heather knows, either. She hasn't said anything. Certainly not to Jade. I'm pretty sure she would have told me. Did Frank say *why* he wanted to call it off? Other than that he was marrying her for the wrong reasons?"

"I don't know. I felt so guilty reading it that I shut it."

"This could be important. I need you to read through it and tell me if there's anything in there about the investigation he was doing."

"I... I can't, Bryce." Her voice grew tight. "It's just too soon. We haven't even buried him yet. I can't read his journal. Why don't I bring it to you first thing in the morning and you can read it."

Bryce hesitated. He really wanted his hands on that journal. Frank might have mentioned something vital about what he was investigating—and whether that something had led to his death. "Okay. If it's not too much trouble." He wasn't sure it would be much easier for him, but he'd do it.

"It's not," she said. "See you soon."

Bryce hung up and pressed his fingers to his eyes, then pulled up Jade's text. Anything new? he asked.

Still waiting.

Should he say anything about Frank having second thoughts about the wedding?

Gotta go. Someone just pulled up.

Bryce closed his eyes to pray. Then opened them and grabbed his keys. Sitting here while Jade put her life on the line just wasn't going to happen.

Jade sat in the command van and kept her eyes on the monitor, watching as a white truck pulled into the parking lot of the warehouse. With the earpiece in her left ear, she could hear the captain's voice like he was standing next to her instead of in one of the unmarked police SUVs now closing in around the perimeter of the warehouse.

"Just got word that Dylan's family is safe and the three men who were watching the house are in custody," the captain said. "I sent officers over there, and they've been waiting for this moment to move in. If we'd tried to do it too soon, we would have tipped off the ring, but the timing was perfect and it went off without a hitch. Everyone is safe. Dylan? You hear that?"

"Yes, sir. Thank you."

"Now it's time to get the rest of them."

Dylan rolled in shortly after the van.

"There he is," Captain Colson said. "Keep eyes on him. And keep the body cams rolling. We do this by the book and take no chances on any lawyers getting these people off."

Affirmatives echoed.

Jade gripped her weapon and made an effort to control her breathing. This was what she was trained for. Hours and hours. Trained to work as a team, to go in and catch the bad guys. To make her hometown a safer place for the people she loved. For her child—and, hopefully, future children. Gage and Jessica's sweet faces flashed in her mind. How she prayed her parents were able to adopt them without any glitches holding things up.

"Let 'em get comfortable," the captain said softly.

The van doors opened, and two men climbed out, then disappeared inside the warehouse.

Tense seconds passed. On the captain's signal, Jade slipped from the command center van behind two team members and together, they scurried to the door. She took up a position on one side, connected eyes with the officer opposite her and nodded. He twisted the knob and pushed the door in. "Police! Everybody on the ground!"

"Show me your hands!"

Jade wasn't sure who called the order as she and the others swarmed inside the building like ants on a hill. She held her weapon in front of her, sweeping it to cover the four men in the back of the warehouse. "Down on the floor!"

Two dropped, and two ran.

Jade bolted after the one closest to her. He darted toward the exit, and she quickly closed the gap. "Police! Stop right there!"

Of course he didn't.

He reached the exit door. Pressed the bar—and went nowhere. The door was locked. Jade slammed into him, knocking the weapon from the back of his waistband. It clattered to the floor and he spun, fist shooting out. She ducked and threw a punch to his solar plexus.

The breath left him and he doubled over. She brought a knee up and caught him in the chin. He cried out and went down. "Stay there and put your hands behind your back."

Wonder of wonders, he did. Jade snapped the handcuffs around his wrists and hauled him to his feet. He swayed, and she kept a grip on him. Looking around, she noted the others were in custody while yet more officers gathered the evidence. It was over. Before the sun came up, she had no doubt the rest of the ring would be captured.

And she and her family would finally be safe.

She directed her prisoner toward the entrance she and the team had breached and stepped outside to see Bryce standing next to her cruiser, Sasha at his side. Her eyes locked on his and her heart thudded a new beat in her chest. How could she still be so attracted to him when their future was still uncertain?

Grief shot through her, making her swallow a gasp. By the time she had the prisoner in the back of the car, she had her emotions under control.

As she shut the back door, locking the man in the back seat, she found herself watching her fellow officers do the same with the other prisoners.

She just had one question. Which one of them had murdered her friend, attacked her and burned her home, and had basically been making her life miserable lately?

She blew out a low breath. Time to find out.

Bryce stayed put, his fears eased at seeing Jade alive and well, doing her job with the confidence of one who was well trained and comfortable with her position. His respect for her just went up another notch—and it was already high to begin with.

Once she had her prisoner situated in the back of her vehicle, she shut the door and walked over to him. "Couldn't stay away, could you?"

"No."

Jade scratched Sasha's ears and gave him a small smile. "I think we got them all," she said. "All of the ones at the top, anyway. I'm sure there are a few low-level stragglers still out there, but we'll catch them soon."

"You think someone will cut a deal?"

She nodded. "I do."

"I was scared for you."

She stiffened and narrowed her eyes. "There's no reason to be. I'm good at what I do."

"I know. You have a dangerous job, but seeing you in action helped me. I might be concerned and pray for your safety, but I don't think I'd be excessively worried you wouldn't come home at the end of the day."

Come home at the end of the day? Heat crept up his neck when he realized the way that sounded. Like they were a couple...or something. She obviously wasn't quite sure how to respond to that and cleared her throat. "Yes, well, that's good. I guess."

"I guess."

He searched for something to say to address his verbal blunder, but before he could think of anything, she patted him on the arm.

"I have to take this guy in," she said.

He blinked. "Oh, I had something else I wanted to run by you. I talked to Lisa."

"And?"

"She found Frank's journal. He kept something like a diary, I guess. Anyway, she said she read some of it. Enough to know that Frank was planning on calling off the wedding."

Jade gasped. "What?"

"So you hadn't heard anything to that effect?"

"Of course not. Does Heather know?"

"I have no idea. I wanted to run this by you before I said anything to her."

"Good. I'm glad you did." She blew out a low sigh. "Okay, let me take care of this guy and then I'll find Heather and ask her what was going on."

"You want me to come with you?"

"No." She bit her lip and paused. "In fact, now that I think about it, I'm not sure I even want to say anything to her. I mean, if she doesn't know, why open that can of worms? Why hurt her like that?"

"Good point."

Jade shook her head. "I'll think on this after I get this guy taken care of. Just don't do anything yet, all right?"

"Of course. Lisa's bringing me his journal first thing in the morning. I'll read though it, and that might give us some more information or insight into what Frank was thinking. Maybe she misunderstood or read something out of context."

"Yes." She grabbed that bit of hope and backed toward the cruiser. "Read it and fill me in."

He nodded. "Be careful."

"Always." She pulled her coat tighter around her neck and grinned. "It feels good."

"What does?"

"One of these guys is probably Frank's killer—and the person after me. I think I'm good to go now."

"Yeah. Still, watch your back until we know for sure, okay?"

"Of course."

Jade climbed into her SUV and glanced in the rearview mirror. Her prisoner glared at her, and she shot him a tight smile. He looked away as she pulled out of the parking lot. At least tonight, the citizens of Cedar Canyon didn't have to worry about a drug ring.

Tomorrow might be another story, but tonight the leaders were in jail. It felt good. As she drove, her thoughts turned to the questions just raised by Bryce.

Frank was going to call off the wedding? Why? Had he met someone else? Surely not. Then—again—why? And had Heather known about Frank's cold feet?

No way. Heather would have told her. Right?

Then again, like Bryce said, it could have just been a misunderstanding on Lisa's part. She continued to mull over what the right thing to do would be. Ask Heather...

or not? By the time she had her prisoner processed into the jail, she still hadn't come to a decision.

But it sure was nice not to have to look over her shoulder anymore.

At least until she caught sight of the headlights in her rearview mirror. They were closing in—and fast.

Jade frowned, tension threading from one shoulder to the next. The driver was going way too quickly. She flipped on her blue lights and slowed. The headlights grew brighter, and her stomach dipped as she realized the person was going to hit her. She jammed the gas pedal and shot forward. However, the car behind her stayed right on her tail.

And then the lights disappeared.

"What are you doing?" she whispered.

The slam into her rear bumper threw her forward against her seat belt, and she hit the brakes out of reflex. The wheel spun under her grip and the SUV whipped sideways. She jerked against the seat belt and slammed her head on the window. Stars flashed. The vehicle tilted on two wheels then crashed onto the asphalt.

Stunned, she hung suspended by the seat belt. Her only thought was that she and her fellow officers had somehow missed a drug dealer. The most important one had gotten away. The one who wanted her dead.

# FOURTEEN

Bryce stood with Captain Colson, who insisted he go over everything Frank had initially told him when he'd asked him to investigate the four officers—including Colson. He wanted to know why Frank had him on the list.

"I don't know. He never said how he picked his suspects." The man didn't seem terribly bothered by it. He seemed more curious than anything—which Bryce could understand. "It could have had something to with your more than usual involvement in the case."

"I was staying on top of it because the commander asked me to—and because I knew the kid who's still in the ICU." His jaw worked. "This is something this town hasn't dealt with before. Don't get me wrong. I know we have our share of drugs running in and out, but this ring…it was killing our kids, and that had to stop. So, yeah, I've been vigilant in keeping up with every last detail pertaining to the investigation."

"I understand."

The captain's radio chirped, and a voice came over the airwaves. "That's dispatch." He pressed the button. "Go ahead. Over."

"Officer down on Gowen Road. Officer down. Be on the lookout for a black Tahoe, license plate ending in 09."

"Who is it? Over."

"Jade Hollis."

Everything in Bryce stilled for a split second before he grabbed his keys from his pocket and gave Sasha's leash a yank. "Sasha, car!"

She responded to his urgency, and they bolted toward his vehicle with the captain's voice ringing in his ears.

Once he was on the road, headed in Jade's direction, he directed his phone to call Jade.

For once the voice command actually worked and the call went through. His heart hammered in his chest while fear sucked the air from his lungs. *Pick up, pick up.*

On the last ring before voice mail, the line clicked. He heard a groan. "Jade? Jade!"

"Ugh. I'm here."

Relief crashed over him. "Are you okay?"

"Trying to figure that out. I'll let you know in a minute."

"I'm almost there. Only a couple of minutes out. So are other officers. I was with Captain Colson when the call came in about an officer down and then dispatch said your name—" He stopped and sucked in a breath. Later. He could deal with his terror later. All that mattered was she'd answered her phone and was talking to him. Breathing air. Still alive. "Stay on the phone with me."

"I'm trapped in my seat belt. I need to get out of it."

"Don't hang up."

"I won't. You're on speakerphone."

He heard rustling. A grunt. Then a thud. "Jade?"

"I'm okay," she gasped. "Just had a bit of a hard landing when I released my seat belt."

The picture that statement presented didn't help his worry. And then he saw her up ahead. He pressed the gas pedal and heard sirens behind him. The sight of her SUV on its right side sent a wave of nausea crashing over him. But she was on the phone. She was okay. "I'm here."

"I've got the window rolled down and am getting ready to climb out. Driver's side."

Her head popped up and he pulled in beside her as she pulled herself out of the window and slid down the roof to the ground.

Bryce captured her into a quick hug before stepping back to check for injuries. Hopefully, the fact that she was able to climb out meant she wasn't hurt too badly. "You've got a cut on your forehead."

"And likely a bruise from the seat belt is going to show up and look lovely."

"I think it's time to start wrapping you in bubble wrap or body armor or something."

She grimaced but didn't argue.

Police cruisers pulled in, and officers surrounded them. Concern for Jade was obvious, and Bryce could see the close bond she had with her fellow officers. He flashed briefly to that remembered camaraderie he used to share with the buddies he'd served with. After the explosion and the loss of his leg, he'd shoved them all away and cut himself off. He'd think about the regret later. "How did this happen?" he asked.

"Guy ran me off the road."

"But…why?"

"I don't know. Trust me, I've been going over and over this in my head. The only thing I can think of is that we missed someone in the sting."

"Then the person who wants you dead is still out there."

"Apparently." She raked a hand through her ponytail, and Bryce noted several cuts and scrapes.

"You need to go to the hospital and get checked out."

"I'm fine. I just need to go to my parents' house and get cleaned up."

He started to argue with her, then snapped his lips shut. He didn't blame her for not wanting to go to the hospital, but that meant he'd need to keep a close eye on her. "You're going to insist on staying at your parents' place, aren't you?"

"Of course."

"Of course. Then I'm letting the captain know you still need protection."

Jade's eyes popped open and she rolled over, stifling her groan. More aches and pains. Would she ever know what it felt like to be pain-free again? The paramedics had taped the cut on her forehead, declared her concussion-free, and told her to be careful.

Be careful. Yes, she would do that.

She sniffed. Bacon and coffee. Two of her favorites. Bryce must be cooking. Now that was a man her mama would tell her was worth keeping. She smiled, then frowned. The problem was, she didn't know if he was even interested in them having a long-term relationship outside of his desire to see Mia. She *thought* he might, but he held himself so distant most of the time, it was hard to tell. Of course his concern was touching, and he did seem to care about her like any friend would, but could it be more? The other question was…what did *she* want? Did she even want more?

It didn't take long to come up with *that* answer. *She* wanted a happily-ever-after—with Bryce. But the truth was, until they found the person who was trying to kill her, it was probably not the best time to think about it anyway.

She checked her phone. A text from Heather. I heard what happened last night. Are you all right?

Jade tapped her response. I'm basically in one piece. That's a positive.

Glad to hear it.

Same here. How are you?

I'm functioning.

Jade frowned and dialed her friend's number. She liked texting for short things, but not for this.

Heather answered on the third ring. "Hey."

"Heather, I'm just going to get to the point. I'm worried about you."

"Well, that makes two of us."

"I'm going to come by and see you. Hang out a bit. Talk. Don't talk. Whatever you want. I just don't want you to be alone."

"I appreciate that, but I'm in the middle of painting and don't want to stop."

"What are you painting?"

"My next masterpiece." She sighed. "Ah, Jade, I don't know. I appreciate the offer, but I'm struggling and I don't want to deal with people right now."

Hurt slammed her. "Deal with *people*? Heather, this is *me* we're talking about. One of your best friends and *partner*. Since when did I get lumped into the 'people' category?"

Heather's silence confounded her. Jade tried to let the slight go. Her friend was hurting and not thinking clearly. One reason she wanted to go see her. "When's his funeral?" she finally asked.

"Lisa's taking care of that. I told her I simply couldn't do it."

The dead sound in her friend's voice scared her. "I'm coming over."

"No. Please. Just give me my space. And time. Everyone deals with grief differently. You know me. You know how I deal with it."

Indecision warred within her. Would it actually help her friend to know that Frank had planned to call off the wedding? Or would it just devastate her even further? Make her question their whole relationship? Or would the anger she'd no doubt feel give her fuel to fight back? Or would she just be terribly confused and hurt and spiral into a depression she might never come back from? Jade just didn't know. Just because *she'd* want to know didn't mean Heather would.

Then again...

"Heather, did you know—" No, now wasn't the time. If ever.

"Know what?"

"Nothing. Just...were you and Frank okay?" The question burst from her lips before she could pull it back in.

"What?"

"Were you guys getting along or were you having some problems?"

"Why are you asking me that?"

Jade bit her lip. "I'm just wondering."

"Did Frank say something to you?"

"Not a thing." Which was completely true. "Look, forget it. Go back to your painting and I'll check on you tomorrow."

"No, I want to know why you'd ask me that."

Her phone vibrated. "I'll have to call you back. I need to get this other line."

"Jade—"

"Sorry, Heather, I need to answer this."

"Fine, but call me back and explain your question."

She hung up, her heart heavy. As much as she wanted to fix this for Heather, she couldn't.

Her phone buzzed for the third time. Not a call after all. It was Bryce texting her from the other room. Breakfast will be ready in ten.

Then so will I.

Ready to eat, then face another day of searching for a killer. And pulling her foot out of her mouth. She'd have to think about what to say before talking to Heather again.

Bryce set the food on the table, feeling very...weird— and wishful. Over the years he'd thought about his future, of course, and had always pictured himself married—but to someone who was like him and didn't want children. At least, he used to think about it before losing part of his leg, but in the past five years, he hadn't allowed himself to dream or hope that he would find someone.

Until he'd seen Jade again. And then he'd learned about Mia and that's all he could picture when he thought about the years ahead—having a life with them. He placed his hands on the counter, dropped his chin to his chest and closed his eyes. He had no business thinking that. She didn't deserve a disabled man.

*Disabled? Maybe by the medical definition, but in*

*his case, he could be honest with himself and say he was only as handicapped as he allowed himself to be.*

His jaw tightened as Titus's voice floated through his mind.

The familiar self-pity threatened to creep over him. "No, no, not going back there," he muttered.

"Bryce? You okay?"

Jade's voice snapped his head up. He cleared his throat. "Yeah. Just…thinking."

"Anything you want to share?"

"Not right now, thanks. You hungry?" He pointed to the table. "We've got eggs, bacon, waffles and grits."

"Starving." She studied him for a moment, and he wondered if she'd insist on him sharing his thoughts. She didn't. Instead, she gave him a slow nod, walked to the coffeepot and poured herself a mug of the steaming brew before settling herself at the table. "This looks amazing. Where did you learn to cook like this?"

The tension in the back of his neck eased a bit. "Thanks. I like to eat, so cooking became a matter of survival." He smiled. "I found all of the food in your mom's refrigerator. I didn't think she'd mind me using it to feed you."

"Of course not. That's what it's there for."

"Your watchdog is out front."

She nodded. "I figured."

His phone buzzed. "That's Lisa. She's going to bring me the journal. I'm going to meet her at the interstate exit so she doesn't have to come all the way into town. I'll only be about thirty minutes or so. Will you be all right until I get back?"

"Sure."

"You want to ride with me?"

"I think I'm going to go see Heather."

"Not alone."

"No, I'll take the officer with me." She finished off the bacon and leaned back to sip her coffee. "She keeps telling me to leave her alone, that she wants to grieve her own way. On the one hand, I understand that. On the other, I think she needs someone there for her—whether she likes it or not."

"I think you're right."

"Well, that's a relief, because I really wasn't sure it was a good idea."

He reached over and squeezed her fingers. "You're a good friend, Jade."

As soon as the words passed his lips, he wanted to pull them back in.

Her eyes shadowed, but she smiled. "A good friend, huh? Well, I try." She slid her hand away from his and stood while Bryce mentally kicked himself all over the place.

*A good friend? A good friend? I'm an idiot.*

"Jade, you're a good friend to Heather. That's all I meant."

"So, not to you."

Heat crept into his cheeks. "Yes, of course you are. I simply meant— I didn't mean… Aw, man." He stood, slipped his hands around her biceps and pulled her against him. A gasp whispered from her, but she didn't pull away. "I'm glad we're friends Jade, but—"

"But what?"

"But…this." He lowered his lips to hers and gave her a moment to protest if she decided she didn't want the embrace to continue. When she wrapped her arms around his neck, he deepened the kiss and realized how right it felt to hold her. Like she was supposed to be there. Her soft lips yielded and he explored gently, hoping his heart came through and she understood it without him having to put it into words.

When he lifted his head, her eyes opened and she watched him. He saw the questions burning there and swallowed hard. Because he didn't have the answers yet. He just knew he wasn't ready to lose her. "I guess I need to get going."

"I guess I do, too."

"You're more than a friend, Jade, but I—"

"But you what?"

"I'm not—" How did explain without sounding like an idiot? Again. "I can't—" Nope. "I'll talk to you later. Be safe."

She frowned but nodded. "You, too."

He hit the door not quite at a run, but pretty close to it.

Once on the porch, he drew in a ragged breath. She was getting under his skin. He laughed. Who was he kidding? There was no *getting* about it. She was already there. So, what was he going to do? The honorable thing by letting her go so she could find someone without so much baggage attached? Or be selfish and try to win her heart? That kiss had told him a lot about what he *wanted* to do, but he could use help struggling with the issue of what he *should* do. And then there was Mia. He knew without a shadow of a doubt he wanted to be in his daughter's life, but the uncertainty and insecurities strangled him.

The indecision was killing him, but he had to meet Lisa and get Frank's journal. Maybe there was a clue in there as to who killed him—or why he wanted to call off the wedding.

If not, then Bryce was at a loss as to what to do next. He just wanted this mystery about Frank to be over. Because when it was over, he and Jade had a lot to talk about.

# FIFTEEN

Jade watched Bryce's taillights disappear around the curve in the long driveway, her thoughts on that kiss. Kind of surprised she could think. Because it had been a really good, *mind-blowing* kiss. Her heart still pounded, and she let out what little breath was in her lungs.

Wow.

Just…wow.

The connection they'd discovered that day at the college wasn't a fluke, and she found herself wanting to explore the possibilities of it more and more each time she saw him. But…while he was obviously attracted to her—and had definitely enjoyed the kiss—something was still eating at him, holding him back emotionally.

The fact that she was the mother of his child? Or something else? Or a combination of the two?

Whatever it was, she needed to figure it out—or simply ask him—before things progressed, because she was on the cusp of falling in love with him.

Okay, it was too late. She was already there. The admission shook her, and she decided she needed to talk things over with someone. Usually, that someone would be Heather, but would that be completely insensitive, to talk to her friend when she'd just had her own happily-ever-after smashed to smithereens? Or would it be a small slice of old normal in the midst of Heather's new normal?

"Ahhh! Too much thinking, Jade. Just go over there and play it by ear. See what feels right." The short pep talk helped.

Her phone buzzed. A text message from one of the detectives involved in the questioning of the four people arrested with the drug ring.

In spite of some pretty compelling incentives to roll over on their buddies—especially the one after Jade—none of the four prisoners had anything. And she believed they were telling the truth.

Which left Jade terribly confused.

Are you sure? she texted.

Not a hundred percent, of course, but it's my gut feeling.

A gut Jade was inclined to trust. She sighed, grabbed a to-go coffee cup and filled it with the hot brew. She added two sugars and one cream and walked outside. Tom Williams leaned against his cruiser, tapping his phone screen. He looked up as she approached. "Tom, how are you this morning?"

"I'm all right. How are you feeling?"

"Beat up and very sore."

He quirked a small smile of compassion at her. "Sorry about that, but it could be worse."

"Much." She handed him the cup of coffee. "How are the kids?"

He smiled. "They're great." He waved the phone at her. "Just letting my wife know I won't be home for lunch. Darryl plans to take over around two for me."

"Oh, I'm sorry you're having to change your plans for me."

"It's okay. It happens."

"I know that for sure. So... I need to go see Heather. I'm worried about her."

He opened the driver's door. "And I get to be your escort."

"More like my chauffeur, if you don't mind. I could drive my car, but if you'll just take me, I won't worry about it."

"Happy to do it." He lifted the cup of coffee. "I take bribes."

"Be careful where you say those words."

"Aw, you know I'm kidding."

"I know. I'll be ready in about ten minutes."

"I'll be here."

True to his word, when she walked out ten minutes later, he was waiting. She climbed into the passenger seat and kept a watch on the mirrors while he drove.

"That's crazy about Dylan, huh?"

"Yeah." She really didn't want to talk about it.

"I never would have suspected it."

"I know. Me either."

"Are they any closer to figuring out what happened to Heather's fiancé?"

Another topic she didn't want to discuss. "No, not yet. I know they're interrogating the people from the drug ring that Dylan was involved with, but so far, no one seems to know anything—and if they do, they're not saying."

"Yeah." He fell silent. "I knew Frank a little."

"When'd you meet him?"

"At the precinct picnic back in September. Seemed like a really nice guy."

"He was."

She fell silent, remembering the afternoon he was referring to. It had been a hot day with lots of food and laughter. She'd only been with the force for about six months at that point. About as long as Heather and Frank had been engaged.

"You went to high school with him?"

"Frank, Bryce, Heather and I were all best friends. We did everything together. People thought we were couples, but we weren't. We just enjoyed hanging out."

"I was a couple of years ahead of you guys."

She remembered Tom from the football team and had always thought he was a handsome guy, but he'd been surrounded by cheerleaders and the popular kids. She was surprised he even knew who she was—other than being on the police force with him.

Tom pulled to a stop in front of Heather's house, and she blinked out of the memories. The windows and front door were open and Jade frowned. Then realized Heather had to be painting. But with what?

She opened the car door.

"I'll be waiting," Tom said.

Jade hesitated. "I can get Heather to run me home so you don't have to miss lunch with your family."

"And leave you unprotected?"

Jade laughed. "I'm a cop and so is Heather. With her watching my back, I'll be fine." And it would be incentive to get Heather out of the house. "Seriously. I'll just tell her she has protective duty."

He still seemed unsure.

"Or stay here," she said. "It never hurts to have another pair of eyes."

He nodded. "I'll just stick around."

"Fine." Jade climbed from the vehicle and shut the door. She took a deep breath and headed for Heather's open front door.

* * *

Bryce pulled into the parking lot of the gas station where they'd agreed to meet.

The place was a beehive of activity, but he spotted Lisa parked to the side out of the way of the gas trucks and the traffic coming and going from the store. Sasha sat in the back, her head resting on Bryce's shoulder. When he slowed, she lay down on the back seat, her eyes watchful and curious. "Stay here, girl. I'll just be a few minutes."

He got out of his truck and walked toward Lisa, catching a glimpse of her through the driver's window. Three steps closer and he could see she was holding something and crying. Two more steps and he could see the item was a small book. Frank's journal, no doubt.

He rapped on the glass and she opened the door to step out. "I got to thinking about what you said. That Frank may have left some kind of a clue about what he was investigating. I read a little more. He not only wanted to call of the wedding, he was concerned about Heather's mental state."

"What do you mean?"

"Apparently when he told her he wanted to postpone the wedding, she went crazy. Yelled at him that he'd never loved her and that this was just the first step in backing out of the wedding. He wrote that he really hadn't meant it to come across that way, but once she verbalized it, it hit him that she was right."

"But why?"

Lisa shook her head and swiped a stray tear. "I haven't gotten to that part—if he even put it in there." She sniffed and handed him the book. "Maybe you can figure it out. I can't read anymore. I wish I hadn't read that. I'm sorry I'm such a wimp."

Bryce sighed and pulled her into a hug for a moment. "It's okay, Lisa. Really. I'll take it from here."

She nodded and scrubbed her palms under her eyes. "I need to visit my friend, then get back home. I left the kids with a neighbor who'll probably be ready to give them back by the time I'm finished."

"They're great kids."

She smiled. "And you're a great friend. Thank you. For everything."

"Of course." He hesitated. "Do you want me to tell you anything I find out in here?"

"Only if you think it will help for me to know it."

"Okay. Sounds fair."

Once he'd seen Lisa back into her car and on the road toward home, Bryce climbed back into his driver's seat and buckled up. He dialed Jade's number and let it ring while he opened the little black journal that held his friend's last thoughts.

# SIXTEEN

Jade had stepped inside Heather's home and immediately been hit by the fumes—and the color of the room. A deep red covered the walls and Jade closed her eyes for a moment. *Lord, please be with Heather. She's hurting so terribly bad.* "Heather? You here?"

Where else would she be? The bathroom? The back bedroom? She knew Heather had used her spare bedroom as a studio when she had been painting before. Maybe she'd started using it again.

The couch had been pushed away from the wall and was covered with a black tarp. The floors that had once been a pretty taupe colored carpet were now just plywood.

What was Heather doing? "Heather!"

Jade's phone rang and she realized it had been ringing for several seconds. She snatched it. "Bryce."

"Hey, how are you doing?"

"I'm at Heather's. Let me call you back in a bit."

"Okay, I just wanted to let you know that I've got the journal. Listen, I'm real concerned about Heather's mental state. Frank was worried, too. It was one reason he wanted to postpone the wedding."

Jade shot a glance toward the hallway. Still no sign

of her friend. She lowered her voice. "Postpone, not call off?"

"Calling it off apparently came later. But she knew and she was extremely upset."

"She knew." And she hadn't said a thing to Jade—or anyone else.

"Listen, watch your back with her."

Jade huffed a short laugh. "You're kidding, right? This is Heather."

"I know. And she's been through a lot. She may not be thinking clearly."

Well, that was true enough. "What exactly does his journal say?"

"I haven't read it yet. I'm paraphrasing what Lisa told me. I'm heading back to town and should be there in about twenty minutes. I'll read some more and try to get the full picture."

"Okay. I'll call you and let you know how it goes here."

He hung up, and Jade walked toward the back of the house. "Heather?" Worry churned within her. Heather had known Frank wanted to call off the wedding. Had she kept quiet because she had hopes he would change his mind? Or…what?

Footsteps in the hallway reached her, and Heather rounded the corner to enter the den, paintbrush in hand, towel over her shoulder. "Ah! Jade?" She pressed a hand to her heart then pulled an AirPod from her ear. "You scared me to death. What are you doing here?"

"I came to check on you. I've been calling your name for the past few minutes. I guess I know why you didn't answer." She let her gaze roam the room. "You've been busy."

"You told me to paint."

"This wasn't exactly what I had in mind, but..."

"It's a horrible color, isn't it?" Heather set the paint-brush on the tarp covering the sofa and rubbed her eyes. "I don't know what I was thinking." She gave a small laugh. "Frank hated the color."

"So, why?"

"Because it would have made him mad." She looked away, then back, fury darkening her eyes. "He was going to call off the wedding."

"I heard."

Heather blinked. "You did?"

"Lisa found his journal and read a bit of the entry where he said he was calling it off."

Her face paled. "Lisa had it? You've got to be kidding me."

"So, you knew about the journal?"

Her friend hesitated. "Yes, but he never intended anyone to read it. Those were his private thoughts and feelings." Heather raked a hand over her hair, pushing a few strands behind her ear. "I can't believe he left it with her."

"He didn't intentionally leave it with her."

"But he did, and she found it and read it, right?" A short scoff. "What else did he say?"

"I don't know. I don't think Lisa read the whole thing, just that part. She gave the journal to Bryce this morning."

"And has he read it?"

"No, he just picked it up. Forget the journal. Why didn't you tell me?"

"Because it was embarrassing!" Heather paced to the kitchen and back. She stopped at the bookshelf she'd moved away from the wall and picked up a picture of her and Frank. "I'd already been left at the altar once, and now this? I couldn't believe it. I thought he was finally—"

"Finally what?"

"Nothing! It doesn't matter now." She replaced the picture and looked down at her hands. "Excuse me a minute while I go wash this paint off."

"Heather—"

"Just give me a minute, Jade, okay?"

Jade raked a hand through her ponytail. "Fine. Sure." Heather disappeared down the hall, and Jade walked to the couch, then back to the front door, her rubber-soled shoes quiet on the plywood. She returned to the couch and dropped her face into her palms.

When she opened her eyes, she spotted something on the plywood that didn't look like it belonged there. A large brown stain.

Coldness settled in the pit of her stomach, and she didn't like where her mind went. But she couldn't help it. She'd seen stains like that before. Jade walked into the hallway and heard the sink in the hall bathroom still running. She hurried to the kitchen and retrieved a plastic baggie and a pointed knife.

Kneeling at the edge of the stain, she stuck the tip of the knife into it, carved out a small sliver of the wood and slid it into the baggie. Then she pinched the edges shut and stuffed the bag into the inside pocket of her jacket.

"What are you doing?"

Jade spun. Heather stood at the entrance to the den, drying her hands on a towel.

"Nothing." She stepped forward trying to hide the knife on the floor. "Just trying to figure out your vision for this room."

Her friend's gaze dropped to the floor, and her jaw

tightened. She tossed the towel onto the covered sofa and shoved her hands into the pockets of her painting smock.

"Why did Frank want to call the wedding off, Heather?" Jade asked. "I thought things were great with you guys."

Heather narrowed her eyes and barked a bitter laugh. "You really don't know."

"I really don't know, so why don't you quit being so vague and fill me in?"

"He wanted to call off the wedding because he was in love with you!"

Jade froze. Her heart pounded. Disbelief coursed through her veins. With eyes locked on Heather's, she shook her head. "No. That's not true. We were just friends."

"You're so naive."

"Heather," Jade said softly, "did you kill Frank?" Heather's left hand rose fast, and Jade found herself staring at the weapon in it. "How could you?" she whispered.

"I didn't want to," Heather said, "but he gave me no choice. He didn't even have the decency to tell me himself. I had to read it in his journal."

"What?"

"He left it sitting on his kitchen table. I thought I'd sneak a peek and see what I might get him for a wedding gift. Only you can imagine how surprised I was to find out he didn't want to get married after all because he was in love with you."

Jade shook her head. It couldn't be true. "He never gave the first clue that he felt anything more than friendship for me."

"And get this," Heather said as though Jade hadn't spoken. "He only asked me to marry him because he felt sorry for me for getting jilted. I almost took that book and threw it at him, but decided not to let him know right off that I knew. I didn't know what I was going to do, but I wasn't going to just sit by and let him humiliate me." She swiped a tear, but her eyes remained hard, and Jade was starting to believe her friend, her partner, the woman she'd entrusted her life to numerous times, might actually kill her.

"Frank cared about you. He always did."

"*Cared* about me? He was supposed to *love* me!" A sob slipped from her and she drew in a slow breath. "He came back the next day after asking me to marry him and said he'd made a mistake. He actually apologized and said he shouldn't have done that. While he felt sorry for me, he couldn't marry me. The problem is, I'd already told my mother and grandmother. I begged him to let it play out for a few months, then if he wanted to call it off, I'd agree. I thought surely I could make him fall in love with me by then. When he kept up the charade, I thought I'd succeeded—except when you were around. You want to know something else he said in his journal? Just before he walked in the room, I read that the more he thought about the engagement, the more he thought it might bring you to your senses, that you'd see what you were losing and ask him to reconsider."

"What?" Jade couldn't help the sharp cry.

"As we got closer and closer to the wedding, Frank's cold feet turned into frozen blocks of ice—and so did his heart."

Jade wasn't sure what to say, how to react—or even what to think. Most of her attention was on the gun in Heather's steady grip. "I'm so sorry," Jade said. "I really am, but please put the gun down and we'll work something out."

A sigh slipped from Heather. "If it was anyone but you saying those words, I might go for it. But I know you, *partner*, and I know 'working something out' means me going down for Frank's murder. And that's not going to happen."

Bryce's heart pounded. He'd pulled into the parking lot of the office he'd rented but hadn't set foot in since returning to Cedar Canyon, to sit in the car and read through just a bit of Frank's journal.

When he read, "I have regrets. A lot of them," his blood pounded and his lungs tightened. Sasha moved closer and nudged him. "It's all right, girl. Give me a minute."

"The biggest being I kept a secret from a friend," Frank had written. "Jade asked me to have Bryce contact her, but I knew why she wanted to talk to him so bad. He's Mia's father. If he comes back, I'll lose Mia and Jade forever. It's wrong of me, I know that. I should tell him, but it's been five years. Almost six. How do I tell him after all this time?" Another entry. "He's coming home. It won't be long before he'll run into Jade and learn about Mia. Once Jade sees him, she'll tell him. And they'll figure out that I've lied to both of them. I'm a horrible friend. I've got to come clean and pray everyone can forgive me, but how can they?" One more. "I know that if I have more time, I'll be able to win Jade's heart. I want to love Heather, but I don't. It's Jade. It's always been Jade, but how do I break that to Heather? I've really messed up and don't see a way out that won't hurt a lot of people." Last one. "Heather's changed. I'm not sure what's going on with her, but there's no way we're getting married. I just need to man up and tell her. Soon. Because Jade isn't showing any inclination that my getting married is bothering her in the least. I think she may be a lost cause. Regardless, I still can't marry Heather.

I'm telling her tonight. She's not going to take it well, and frankly, she's been so unstable lately, I'm worried about what she might do."

He'd read enough to know that Jade could very possibly be in danger. He dialed her number and set the phone in the mount on his dash while the Bluetooth kicked in.

When it rang four times before going to voice mail, he put the SUV in Reverse and backed out of the parking spot, worry for Jade making his palms sweat. Heather's house was only about five minutes from him.

Unfortunately, a lot could happen in five minutes.

# SEVENTEEN

"If you shoot me," Jade said, keeping her voice even, "Tom will hear. He's sitting outside." Her phone had been vibrating in her pocket, but Heather didn't seem to hear it. All she could do was pray it was Bryce, and when she didn't answer, he would come to investigate.

"Tom?" Heather asked.

"Tom Williams. With the wife and two kids. He brought me here because the captain assigned someone to be with me at all times, thanks to you trying to kill me. If you pull the trigger and he comes running in, you'll have to kill him, too. Do you really want more deaths on your conscience?" Because it was obvious killing Frank was eating away at her. "The ME said Frank never saw it coming, but he was shot by someone he was facing," Jade said softly. "How did it happen, Heather? Did he just stand there and let you put two bullets in him?"

"I don't want to talk about it."

"Well, I do! It's my life we're talking about here. And Frank's! And the kids'! What if Mia had been home when you set my house on fire?"

"I figured she'd stay with your parents. She always does these days."

"But what if she hadn't? You could have killed her."

"Well, she's not dead, so drop it!" Heather's eyes flashed desperation, and that scared Jade almost as much as having the gun aimed at her. "Wait a minute. How did you get the bombs in there and then disappear so quickly? There was no car, nothing, but I know I saw you out near the barn."

Heather shuddered. "That was a close one."

"So, I did see you!"

"I thought for sure you'd find me."

"But where—" She broke off. "Our secret place in the loft," she whispered. "That's how you were coming and going without anyone noticing you."

"It was a simple thing to grab a horse from the pasture and bareback it up to the barn. No car necessary. No sounds to alert anyone."

"And you know my family's schedule so you could plan around it." So stupid. She and Bryce had talked about the secret place and she hadn't even *looked*. Because no one had known about it and it was almost impossible to find unless one knew it was there. Like Heather did.

"Check on Tom," Heather said. "Is he sitting in the car or outside of it?"

Jade went to the window and peered out, wishing there was some way she could signal the man she needed help. But he wasn't watching the house. He was sitting in his car, talking on his phone. "Inside."

"Call him in here."

"What? Why?"

"He brought you here. I can't exactly explain why he's not taking you anywhere."

She planned to kill him and Jade—and probably anybody who tried to stop her. "Is that what you did to

Frank? Call him over here and when he walked in, shot him?"

"Yes! I mean, no! Argh!" Heather drew in a deep breath. "Yes, I asked him to come over. We talked and he wouldn't listen to reason. He said he was calling off the wedding and that was that. I couldn't let him do that. Don't you understand? I couldn't let him!"

"So you shot him." Jade could picture it playing out. "And then...what? How'd you get him into your car?"

"He was still alive," she whispered. "I was going to take him to the hospital. He got up on his feet and I got him in the car and he died."

"And you had to hide the evidence." And no one would have searched Heather's car.

"I drove his car home, got a shirt to put on him because there was so much blood. I couldn't drive him around like that. Then I walked back here, changed his shirt and drove him to the mill. I buried him right where they found him, but I still had to do something with his bloody jersey."

"And you were burying it when I showed up."

"Yeah," she said softly.

"Why didn't you just bury it with him?"

"Because I just...didn't. I'd left it in the car and only found it when I went to leave. I was almost finished when you showed up." Her eyes clouded. "To ruin things once again."

"Heather, I—"

"Enough. Get Tom in here."

Jade's mind spun and she tried to think and plan. "No. I won't put him in danger."

"It's too late, Jade." She blinked away tears. "If only you hadn't come back. You should have stayed away. Get him in here!"

Arguing with her wouldn't do any good. Jade took note of the layout of the kitchen and den area once again. Jade still had her weapon in her holster and her phone in her pocket. A testament to Heather's state of mind that she hadn't had Jade toss them out to her.

"Instead of getting him in here, if I can convince him to leave, will you let him go?"

Heather bit her lip, then sighed. "Yes." She tightened her grip on the gun. "But no funny stuff, Jade. I know you're scrambling for a way out of this. Trust me, there isn't one."

Chills danced up Jade's spine, and dread curled in the pit of her stomach. "You'd do this to Mia? My parents? You'd take me away from them?"

"I'm sorry, I really am, but I'm not going to prison. Now, either get Tom in here or convince him to leave. You have five minutes. Use the phone in your pocket that keeps buzzing and put it on Speaker."

Jade removed the device and dialed Tom's number. "Everything okay?" he asked, his low voice rumbling into the room.

"Everything's fine," she said with a glance at Heather's unrelenting eyes. "Like we discussed in the car, Heather's going to take over protective duty and drive me home. You can leave."

"Now, Jade, you know I can't do that. The captain would have my head."

Jade closed her eyes for a brief second. When she opened them, Heather's granite features hadn't changed. "You know Heather's been going through a tough time. We'll be here a while. I don't want you to miss out on your lunch with your cousin." *Don't give me away, Tom, please.* "Why don't you do that and come back. It's going to bug me to death if I'm the reason you miss out."

For a moment, he didn't answer, and she wondered if he'd remind her that it was his wife and kids he'd planned to lunch with, not a cousin. Then he sighed. "All right, if you're sure. You know Darryl should be here any time now. You want me to let him know not to come?"

"Yes, please. Heather can take me home. She'll have my back while you have a nice steak."

"Right. Talk to you soon."

She disconnected and noted the three missed calls.

"Who's been calling you?" Heather asked.

"Bryce."

"Gotten chummy with him, haven't you? I suppose he's in love with you, too."

The venom in those words slapped Jade in the face. "I never really knew you at all, did I?" she asked. "It must have been so very hard being my partner and pretending to be my friend all this time, but I have to say, you've given an outstanding performance."

Heather's expression never changed. "Is he gone?"

Jade glanced out the window. "Yes."

"Throw your phone over here."

She tightened her fingers around the device, then tossed it onto the sofa.

"Only you would send away your only hope of rescue," Heather said. Her finger tightened, and Jade dove behind the kitchen counter, pulling her weapon from her shoulder holster as she rolled. The crack of Heather's service weapon rang through the house. "I've got my gun out," Jade shouted, "and I *will* shoot you. Put it down!"

"Not a chance." Another shot. One of anger as there wasn't any way that she could have hit Jade.

"How could you, Heather? We were friends. All four of us. You killed Frank and now you're going to kill me?

Bryce is going to figure it out once he reads the journal. Are you going to kill him, too?"

"Don't talk to me about Frank. Do you know he actually said he cared about me and hoped I'd find someone to love me like I deserved to be loved—and that he had to find you and tell you what he'd done and how he felt? And then he was going to ask your forgiveness." A harsh bark of laughter slipped from Heather, and Jade frowned. "I was the one he should have been begging forgiveness from."

"So, what now, Heather? How long can we stay like this?"

"As long as it takes. Because whoever comes to the door looking for you is going to get a bullet."

"Bryce knows I'm here."

"Then Bryce will die unless we're gone before he gets here."

Jade drew in a deep breath and knew she was stuck. She wouldn't put Bryce at risk. Mia needed at least one of them alive. Anger coursed through her at the lives Heather had already turned upside down—and the lives she'd continue to upend if she managed to kill Jade. Even if she was caught and found guilty, Jade would still be dead.

"Jade? I'm not playing around. Slide your gun out here and walk to the front door."

Hearing the resolve in Heather's voice, Jade knew there was no way she was letting Bryce walk in and be confronted by the woman's bullets. She sent up a prayer. "Fine. Let's go." She sent her weapon skidding across the plywood and stood, holding her hands where Heather could see them.

She connected her gaze to Heather's and found no softening of the woman's resolve. Scrambling for a plan, she walked to the front door, and Heather fell into step behind her. Jade didn't have to turn to see the gun still pointed at her back.

Heather stayed close, and Jade figured she was using Jade's body to hide the weapon in case one of her neighbors decided to look out a window. Heather had parked her small Honda in the driveway since she kept a lot of her art supplies in the one-car garage, and with each step toward the vehicle, Jade knew she was going to have to do something.

A horn blasted behind her and she whirled, kicked out and caught Heather's arm with the side of her foot. Heather hollered and went to her knees while the gun spun away from her. Jade lunged and slammed an elbow into Heather's head. The woman screamed but didn't lose her balance. Instead, she threw her body forward and wrapped her hand around the weapon.

"Jade!"

From the corner of her eye, she caught sight of Bryce moving toward her. Time slowed as Heather turned, lifted the weapon and aimed it at Jade. Jade froze, her senses on hyperalert. Movement to her left. A blur flashed in front of her, then slammed into her. She registered the crack of the gun in Heather's hand as the air in her lungs whooshed out.

Another pop from behind her and Heather went down screaming and holding her left shoulder.

"Stay down! Stay down!" Tom's harsh order reached her.

From underneath the heavy body on top of hers, Jade could see Tom approaching, his weapon still aimed at Heather.

With Tom covering Heather, Jade scrambled out from

beneath the crushing weight, heart pounding, blood rushing in her veins. "Bryce!"

He coughed and groaned. Jade ran her hands over him, looking for the bullet wound. His hand covered hers. "Got the vest," he wheezed.

Jade jumped to her feet to see Heather going after the weapon she'd dropped.

"I said stay down!" Tom stopped his approach, and Jade knew she had only a millisecond to act.

She threw herself between Heather and Tom's gun. "Don't shoot her!" Then lunged and punched the woman in her wounded shoulder.

Heather screeched and went down. Jade grabbed the weapon and tossed it out of reach, then flipped Heather on her stomach.

Tom hurried to her side and clapped the handcuffs around Heather's wrists. Jade looked up at him. "Thank you."

He glared. "I understood something was wrong when you said *cousin*. That was smart. However, getting between Heather and me was just plain stupid. I almost shot you."

"I know, but I couldn't let you do it."

His frown deepened, but his eyes flashed understanding. "Ambulance is on the way."

"Good. I'm going to check on Bryce." She scrambled back to him to find him breathing and staring at the sky. "You okay?"

"Yeah, just trying to catch my breath."

She dropped her head to his shoulder. "How'd you know to honk the horn?"

"The way Heather was walking with you. I knew she had a gun on you."

"You saved my life."

His arm stole around her. "I had to. Because I can't imagine living without you. Or even Mia now. Tell me you'll give me a chance to be the kind of father she deserves. I'll do my best to be worthy of her."

Jade kissed him. Hard and swift and with all of the love her heart held for him. "There's nothing I want more. I love you, Bryce."

He hugged her tight. "I don't deserve you," he whispered.

Paramedics descended, and Jade waved them away still lying across Bryce's chest. "Check Heather first."

"We've got paramedics on her. Heard your hero here took a bullet."

"To the vest," Jade said.

"Ma'am, let us check him out, please."

Bryce gripped her fingers. "We're not done discussing things," he said softly.

"Okay."

She moved away, her heart full for the moment. Bryce hadn't said he loved her, but it had been in his eyes. She turned her attention to Heather who lay handcuffed to the gurney.

Just that fast, her emotion flipped into despair. Anger. Betrayal. The paramedics wheeled their patient toward the ambulance while two officers followed. One would ride in the back with her and the EMT.

Heather met her gaze for a brief moment, then looked away. Jade let out a slow breath and turned to find Bryce next to her. He placed an arm across her shoulders and kissed her temple. "It's over," he said. "She killed Frank, didn't she?"

"Yes."

"And she was behind all the attempts on your life?"

"She was."

"I read some of Frank's journal," he said, "and I'll be honest, based on what he wrote, I think Heather needs help more than prison."

"We'll make sure she gets the mental health services, but I don't think there's anything we can do to keep her out of prison."

"Probably not."

"What about you? Are you all right?"

"I've been cleared. Bruised, but not broken."

"You threw yourself in front of that bullet she meant for me," Jade said, her voice thick.

"And I'd do it all over again as long as it meant keeping you safe."

He wanted to be a father to Mia and he'd taken a bullet for Jade. She was pretty sure that meant he loved her. The question was, would he admit it?

Even through all of the chaos and the interruptions, Bryce still heard Jade's voice ringing in his mind. "I love you, Bryce," she'd said. Four words that had thrilled him and scared him to death all at the same time. He was willing to admit he loved her, too, and little Mia had already wormed her way into his heart. In spite of his yearning to be her father, the doubts about his ability to be the kind of father she needed wanted to cripple him.

Jade squeezed his hand, and he returned the pressure. "Let's go," he said.

"Where?"

"Someplace peaceful where we can talk without interruptions."

She smiled. "I know just the place. Let me call Mom and Dad and tell them they can come home. Then we can go."

Two hours later, after promising to give their statements in the morning, Bryce rode Caesar, a beautiful paint with a sweet temperament, and followed Jade to the top of the hill on her parents' property. When she pulled her horse to a stop, he did the same and took in the view. A manmade lake at the bottom of the hill rippled in the wind. Snow covered the rest of the area, but he could almost picture how it would look in the spring. Rolling green meadows, blue skies, wildflowers and trees. "Wow."

"I know. This is the most peaceful place on earth, I do believe."

"I won't argue that." He dismounted, then helped her down even though she didn't need his assistance. He turned her to face him. "Jade, I've been doing a lot of thinking. A lot."

"Uh-oh."

A slight smile pulled at the corners of his lips. "I know I come with a lot of baggage. Some days, I'll admit, I don't even feel like a complete man because of my leg."

A gasp slipped from her. "I hope you know that's not true."

"I do. Mentally. But sometimes my self-pity outweighs my common sense. I can be moody and snarky when that happens." He swallowed and looked away. "I don't know if you understand what that entails."

"I think I have a pretty good idea. I can be that way myself. Everyone can. Life isn't all about smiles and good times—although it's necessary to have those. But it's also knowing you can count on the people you're doing life with, you know?"

He nodded, then pulled her close to kiss her. A sweet, cherished melding of lips and hearts. After a moment, he lifted his head. "I love you, Jade. With everything in me. I think it's only fair that you know that."

"Why do I hear a *but* in there?"

"Only a faint one. I don't want to live my life in fear—or regret not taking chances. I don't want to look back in twenty years wishing I'd done something different. I want a life with you and Mia. I know my PTSD worries you, but if you can bring yourself to trust me—"

She pressed cold fingers to his lips. "I trust you. I trust you with my life. The one you saved not too long ago." A shudder rippled through her at the thought, and he hugged her close, relishing her nearness. A little surprised she wasn't pushing him away. "So, can we tell Mia?"

"As soon as they get home." She glanced at her phone. "Which will be any minute now."

They rode the horses back to the house, and Bryce saw the Harrises' vehicle in the drive. His heart pounded, and anticipation made his hands sweat in spite of the chilly weather.

Mia must have been watching for them, because she burst from the door in an all-out run, launching herself at Jade as soon as her feet were on the ground. "Mama, we're back!"

"I see that."

Mia turned to Bryce. "I'm glad you're here, too."

Bryce could only stare. This beautiful little girl was his.

"Bryce?" Jade asked. "You okay?"

He cleared his throat. "Yeah. I'm okay."

Jade smiled. "Let's go in the barn and have a chat."

"Mr. Bryce, too?"

"Yeah," Jade said, "Mr. Bryce, too."

Once in the barn, Jade and Bryce tied up their horses and quickly pulled the tack from them, then sent them out into the pasture. Jade pulled Mia into her arms and kissed her forehead. Bryce decided he'd never tire of watching the two of them together. The three of them sat on the large hay bales overlooking the land.

"Mia," Jade said, "you know how you've asked me about your daddy and how you wanted to meet him?"

"Uh-huh."

"Well, what would you say if I told you Mr. Bryce was your daddy?"

Mia's eyes went round and she turned her gaze on Bryce. "You're my daddy?"

"I am."

Mia wiggled out of Jade's arms and turned to stand in front of him. "Are you really and truly?"

"Really and truly." Bryce couldn't help the huskiness in his voice.

"Are you going to be here for Christmas?"

He lifted his gaze and locked it on Jade's. "I'm planning on it."

"Cool." She looked at him out of the corner of her eye. "Will you take me fishing?"

Bryce let out a laugh. "Fishing? Sure."

"And will you put the squirmy worm on the hook?"

"Absolutely."

She grinned. "You're a real daddy. Real daddies put the gross worm on the hook for their little girls."

Bryce wasn't sure whether to laugh or not. He caught Jade's gaze once more and saw tears standing in her eyes. As well as a good dose of humor. She smiled and swiped a stray tear. Bryce held his arms out to Mia, and she let him pick her up. "I'll bait any hook you want, kiddo."

She kissed his cheek. "I'm glad you're my daddy."

"I am, too, Mia."

And then he couldn't speak as his emotions threatened to overwhelm him, but Jade slipped a shoulder under his arm, and he held her close while dropping a kiss on Mia's head.

Finally, he managed to push words past his tight throat. "I thought I knew what I wanted and what I didn't want, Jade. The truth is, I had no idea what I really wanted until you told me Mia was mine."

"And this is what you wanted?"

"This is exactly what I wanted. And I'm beyond blessed to have it." He kissed her while Mia giggled. "I just have one thing left to say."

"What's that?"

"I love you."

# EPILOGUE

*Christmas Morning*

Jade slipped down the stairs of her parents' house, her bare feet silent on the cold hardwood, but relishing the feel of it under her toes.

The Christmas tree stood tall in the den, decorated with strands of popcorn and homemade decorations.

She walked over and looked out the window. Her home was gone. First burned, then bulldozed to leave a clean slate for a new building. She should feel devastated, but right now, she simply felt blessed and thankful to be alive. And doubly thankful that her family was safe and here to celebrate this beautiful day with her.

It had snowed last night, and the world of white in the predawn morning greeted her.

Warm hands slid over her shoulders and she smiled, leaning back into Bryce's arms. "How was the guest bed mattress?"

"Comfortable and warm. I appreciate your parents for letting me use it. I really didn't want Mia to beat me to the tree."

She laughed and turned to see Sasha sniff at the gifts under the tree, then lumber over to her gigantic bed near the fireplace. "Sasha feels right at home, doesn't she?"

"Of course."

She turned. "I love you, Bryce."

A sheen coated his eyes for a moment before he blinked. "I love you too, Jade."

Her heart stuttered with gladness before settling down to beat a little faster.

"So, I have a question for you."

Butterflies swirled in her stomach. "What's that?" she asked. He dropped to one knee and Jade sucked in a deep breath. "Bryce…are you doing what I think you're doing?" she whispered.

"Shush, you'll make me mess up the moment."

"I'm shushed."

He grinned and gripped her fingers. "So," he said, "here goes."

"Here goes what?" Just ask already! She kept the shout between pressed lips, but the *yes* was already forming.

"Will you marry me? In spite of my insecurities and doubts? Because while I may have those about myself, the one thing I know for sure is that I don't want to face the future without you and Mia."

She kissed him. Long and hard and until they were both breathless.

When she pulled away, she had to blink to see through the tears.

He swallowed. "Um…so, can I take that as a yes?"

She laughed. "Yes." The word finally burst from her. "Absolutely."

"That was very decisive. Like you know exactly what you want."

"I do. I want you."

"Doesn't get much better than that."

Except when he kissed her again, she decided it actually *could* get better.

"Good morning," a little voice said from behind them.

Jade turned and smiled. Mia stood in the entranceway, one foot on top of the other, her dark hair tangled around her sleep-flushed face. "Good morning, Little Bear," she said. "Where are the twins?"

"They're trying to decide if we're really having Christmas because of the snow."

"Of course we are," Bryce said. "Tell them and your grandparents to come on. We'll open gifts, then I'm making my famous pancakes." He looked at Jade. "If that's okay with your mom."

"I'm sure she'll love it."

"Yum!" Mia spun and raced off. Less than a minute later, the three children returned with Jade's parents in tow. Mia rode piggyback on Gage. He lowered her gently to the floor and stood, mouth open, staring at the tree and the gifts surrounding it. Jessica's expression mirrored his.

"Well?" Jade's father asked. "What are you waiting for? It's Christmas! Let's open presents!"

The kids yelled and darted for the tree. Sasha raised her head, eyeing the chaos. Deciding all was fine, she lowered her protective stance and watched the paper fly. A bow landed on her nose and she huffed a sigh before swiping it off with a paw.

Tears rose in Jade's eyes as she watched her family. Bryce was like a kid himself, taking delight in each wondrous moment and gleeful shout of joy. Her mom and dad eyed all three children, watching and laughing. They'd told Gage and Jessica last night that the adoption would be final after the first of the year, and they'd found their forever home. And forever family.

Finally, Bryce rose and joined her. "You're just taking it all in, aren't you?" he asked.

"I am."

"It's some kind of crazy, isn't it?" He grinned. "I love it." He leaned over to kiss her. "And I love *you*." Tears shimmered in his eyes as Mia ran over to throw herself into his arms.

He caught her easily and lifted her to plant a kiss on her cheek. "What is it, kiddo?"

"Merry Christmas, Daddy."

Jade swallowed a sob as Bryce went still. Then he lowered himself to his knees, the prosthetic not hindering his downward motion. "Merry Christmas, sweetheart. This is the best Christmas I've ever had, and you want to know why?"

"Yes!"

"Because you—and everyone in this room—are a part of it." He hugged her, and Mia reached for Jade to make it a group hug. Sasha rose and made her way over to them, pushing her large head into the midst. Jade's heart swelled to the point of rupturing. Life was never perfect, but it was good, and she was grateful.

"Now, who's ready for pancakes?" Jade said.

More cheers erupted along with more joy, more love, a couple of excited barks, and more memories to cherish.

It was definitely the best Christmas ever.

\* \* \* \* \*

Dear Reader,

Thank you so much for going on this journey with Bryce, Jade and Mia. I hope you fell in love with them as deeply as I did. It's always exhilarating and a bit sad to finish a story—exhilarating in the accomplishment, sad because I'm going to miss watching the characters grow. And Bryce and Jade had a *lot* of growing to do, didn't they? They had a lot to overcome in their struggle to find both a killer and true love! But they persevered through tough odds and emerged victorious. So they got their happy ending, and that's all that really matters, right?

Again, thank you for reading, and I pray that as you overcome the struggles of this world, you'll keep your eye on the "happy ending" that awaits us as believers in eternity.

God bless,
*Lynette Eason*

# WE HOPE YOU ENJOYED THIS BOOK!

*Love Inspired*®
## SUSPENSE

Uncover the truth in these thrilling stories of faith in the face of crime from Love Inspired Suspense. Discover six new books available every month, wherever books are sold!

LoveInspired.com

*Danger has caught up with Ashley Willis, and she'll
have to trust the local deputy in order to stay one step
ahead of a killer who wants her dead.*

*Read on for a sneak preview of*
Secret Mountain Hideout *by Terri Reed,*
*available January 2020 from Love Inspired Suspense.*

*It couldn't be.*

Ice filled Ashley Willis's veins despite the spring
sunshine streaming through the living room windows of
the Bristle Township home in Colorado where she rented
a bedroom.

Disbelief cemented her feet to the floor, her gaze
riveted to the horrific images on the television screen.

Flames shot out of the two-story building she'd hoped
never to see again. Its once bright red awnings were now
singed black and the magnificent stained glass windows
depicting the image of an angry bull were no more.

She knew that place intimately.

The same place that haunted her nightmares.

The newscaster's words assaulted her. She grabbed on
to the back of the faded floral couch for support.

"In a fiery inferno, the posh Burbank restaurant The
Matador was consumed by a raging fire in the wee hours
of the morning. Firefighters are working diligently to
douse the flames. So far there have been no fatalities.
However, there has been one critical injury."

Ashley's heart thumped painfully in her chest, reminding her to breathe. Concern for her friend Gregor, the man who had safely spirited her away from the Los Angeles area one frightening night a year and a half ago when she'd witnessed her boss, Maksim Sokolov, kill a man, thrummed through her. She had to know what happened. She had to know if Gregor was the one injured.

She had to know if this had anything to do with her.

"Mrs. Marsh," Ashley called out. "Would you mind if I use your cell phone?"

Her landlady, a widow in her mideighties, appeared in the archway between the living room and kitchen. Her hot-pink tracksuit hung on her stooped shoulders, but it was her bright smile that always tugged at Ashley's heart. The woman was a spitfire, with her blue-gray hair and her kind green eyes behind thick spectacles.

"Of course, dear. It's in my purse." She pointed to the black satchel on the dining room table. "Though you know, as I keep saying, you should get your own cell phone. It's not safe for a young lady to be walking around without any means of calling for help."

They had been over this ground before. Ashley didn't want anything attached to her name.

Or rather, her assumed identity—Jane Thompson.

*Don't miss*
Secret Mountain Hideout *by Terri Reed,*
*available January 2020 wherever*
*Love Inspired Suspense books and ebooks are sold.*

LoveInspired.com

# Get 4 FREE REWARDS!

## We'll send you 2 FREE Books plus 2 FREE Mystery Gifts.

**Love Inspired® Suspense** books feature Christian characters facing challenges to their faith... and lives.

**FREE** Value Over **$20**